Sherlock Holmes

Have Yourself a Chaotic Little Christmas

By

Gwendolyn Frame

i

Paperback ISBN 9781780923383
ePub ISBN 9781780923390
PDF ISBN '9781780923406

Published in the UK by MX Publishing
335 Princess Park Manor, Royal Drive,
London, N11 3GX
www.mxpublishing.co.uk

Cover design by www.staunch.com

To

everyone who participated in the Sherlockian advent calendar challenge of 2011

Contents

Foreword

What do you get when you take a bunch of wildly imaginative Sherlockians with decent writing skills and you point out that Christmas is coming?

Well, you may not get an advent calendar challenge *every* time, but you certainly got it in 2011.

This book is not a collection of all the stories written for the 2011 advent calendar challenge, because every Sherlockian had her own collection and there were quite a few of us participating. No, these stories are mine. A couple of them you might recognise as having been published in *Tales from the Stranger's Room*. Seven of them weren't in my original collection, because I joined the party a week late.

Remember when I said "wildly imaginative"? I wasn't kidding. Everyone contributed story prompts to the people running the challenge, and I got some prompts that the Great Detective would probably have considered *outré*. Stuff like vampires, Jack the Ripper, graveyard picnics... yes, you really are about to read that.

Fortunately for everyone's blood pressure, I also received more traditional requests regarding minor characters like the Irregulars, the "Twelve Days of Christmas," Mycroft, Mary, Lestrade, etc. Even Moriarty gets his brief time in the limelight!

So here's to my fellow participants, the friend who gave

me a fast grammar check, Holmes and Watson, Jeremy Brett and David Burke (and Eric Porter!), and to the wonderful authors whose works inspired me. Merry Christmas!

Gwendolyn Frame, 2012

Day 1: Their First Christmas

"Holmes, wake up!"

"Mmph!"

"Holmes, come now, old boy—it's *Christmas!*"

"Watson, go back to beeed!"

Doctor Watson grinned like a child who'd discovered a stash of presents. "Can't do that!" he chirped merrily. "I woke up at six, couldn't go back to sleep and waited till half past seven to come down and wake you up."

Sherlock Holmes threw back his covers in shock, grey eyes wide. "Do you mean to tell me that you woke up at *six in the morning of your own freewill?*"

Watson nodded happily.

"Oh, for the love of heaven…" Holmes groaned and disappeared back beneath his covers.

Watson sighed. "Holmes, do come on. It's *Christmas.*"

"Another excuse for waking a man early every twenty-fifth of December," came the muffled retort.

"Dickens," Watson said drily. "I'm impressed." Not to be deterred, he yanked back the covers. Holmes merely tightened up immediately into a ball and buried his face into his pillow.

A positively wicked idea occurred to Watson then, and he shivered at the daringness of it. He stepped quietly out of the bedroom and into the sitting-room, crossing over to one of the windows, which he opened as noiselessly as he could. He shivered again—this time at the icy air—steeled himself and quickly scooped up a handful of snow from the windowsill outside. He hastily shut the window with one hand and dashed back to Holmes's bed, hurrying before his other hand froze. He found that he had to yank the covers back again, did so, and dumped his small load onto the detective's head.

Holmes sat bolt upright with a yelp, by which time Watson was already backing away for the door. "WATSON!"

"MerryChristmasmydearfellow," Watson said in a rush, ducking out of the room and shutting the door behind him. He hurried down the stairs and flung on his coat and scarf, running back up halfway to shout, "I'll be outside if you want to take revenge!" Not waiting for an answer, he took the steps back down two at a time and burst out of the house.

Ten minutes later, he was lying facedown in a snow bank, two thin and deceptively strong hands keeping him there. Of course, he had had no warning whatsoever. "Holmes—*gah!*— Holmes, I'll get frostbite!" The pressure suddenly lifted, and he twisted around, a snowball soon out of his hand and impacting his assailant's chest.

"Oomph!"

"Well, it *is* true," Watson protested at the younger man's evil eye. "I really would... have..." His dignity prevented him from yelling, but it did not prevent him from taking to his heels at the sight of the livid detective.

XXX

When Mrs. Hudson looked out her window to see what all the commotion was about, she saw two young but grown men running about like schoolboys and hurling snowballs at each other. "They'll be catching pneumonia," she muttered, shaking her head. She opened the window and leaned out of it. "Gentlemen, what on earth are you doing?"

Both her tenants stopped and waved. "Merry Christmas, Mrs. Hudson!" Watson called.

"Merry Christmas, Mrs. Hudson!" Holmes echoed, his normally-pale features quite red from the cold.

"Merry Christmas." The good landlady shook her head and closed her window. "Honestly, those two. Just like boys."

XXX

"Here..." Watson pulled the package out from under the small tabletop tree and handed it to Holmes. "Open it."

Holmes looked taken aback. "A Christmas present for me? Watson, you didn't need to do this!"

"I didn't *need* to, but I *wanted* to." Watson shrugged. "Open it."

Holmes tore at the festive wrapping paper, obviously chagrined that he was receiving a present and giving none in return. But his face lit up when he saw the music books lying in his lap. "My *dear* fellow…"

Watson grinned. "Do you like them?"

"*Like* them? Ha!" Holmes looked up with a boyish grin. "My improvisations got to be too much for you, eh, Watson?"

"Oh, no, that's not what I—"

Holmes chuckled and held up a hand. "It's all right, my boy." He looked down at the music and shook his head. "I'm afraid I have nothing to give you in return."

"Seems to me that's rather the point of Christmas."

Holmes looked up sharply, and one corner of his mouth pulled back. "…indeed."

XXX

Watson was curled up in his armchair with *A Christmas Carol* that evening when Holmes opened his violin case and pulled out the Stradivarius. "I may not have a tangible present, Doctor," the detective said solemnly, "but I do have a gift to give you, meagre though it be."

Watson shut the book and smiled. "I believe I can live with that," he said with a smile.

Holmes tucked the Stradivarius under his chin and began to play, the familiar strains of "Silent Night" filling the air. As Watson watched his friend, he knew that Sherlock Holmes was improvising, and it was the most beautiful rendition of the song that he had ever heard.

"Silent night," he sang quietly, hesitantly. He glanced up at the detective in a silent request for permission.

Holmes merely smiled, and Watson smiled back.

Silent night, holy night

All is calm, all is bright

Round yon virgin, mother and Child

Holy Infant, so tender and mild

Sleep in heavenly peace,

Sleep in heavenly peace

The music continued, carol after carol infusing te room with a warm peace it had seldom known. Watson didn't realise he had drifted off until the music faded away and a blanket lay around him. He blinked up sleepily at the smiling face of his friend. "Ho'mes?"

"Go back to sleep, dear fellow," Holmes whispered. "You were up early, don't forget."

Watson was too comfortable and sleepy to argue. "Merry Christmas, Holmes."

"Merry Christmas, Watson."

Day 2: Heroes

"I wonder if we'll ever be put into stories."

Sherlock Holmes glanced at his friend and cocked a quizzical eyebrow. "Do you mean aside from the Lauriston Garden Case?"

"Well, yes," Watson said, rather sheepishly. He cleared his throat before continuing. "I wonder if people will ever say, 'Do you want to hear about Sherlock Holmes, the private consulting detective?' and children will say, 'Yes, those are some of my most favourite stories. Mr. Holmes was really something, wasn't he, Papa?' 'Yes, my boy, the greatest man of his time'— and you know that's saying quite a bit."

Holmes barked a sharp but merry laugh. "You seem to have left out the other protagonist—the good Doctor. 'I want to hear more about Dr. Watson.'" His expression grew solemn and earnest as he met his friend's hazel gaze. "'Mr. Holmes would not… *could* not have got very far without him.'"

"Holmes," Watson murmured. "You shouldn't joke that way—I was being serious."

Sherlock Holmes smiled fondly. "So was I, my dear Watson."

Day 3: Home at Last

He hurried out to the deck, a cool breeze brushing his face as he opened the door. There she was. London.

Grinning like a fool, he threaded his way through the press of people and reached the railing, gripping it and leaning forward. The breeze ruffled his silver-shot hair gently, and he closed his eyes and threw his head back, enraptured.

He was *home*.

The memories flooded waking thought like a rushing torrent, and he made no effort to stay them.

> *"You have been in Afghanistan, I perceive."*

> *"I should like to see him clapped down in a third-class carriage on the Underground, and asked to give the trades of all his fellow-travellers. I would lay a thousand to one against him."*

> *"Your merits should be publicly recognised. You should publish an account of the case. If you won't, I will for you."*

> *"It may be that you are not yourself luminous, but you are a conductor of light. Some people without possessing genius have a remarkable power of stimulating it. I confess, my dear fellow, that I am very much in your debt."*

"That is why I have chosen my own particular profession, or rather created it, for I am the only one in the world."

"Miss Morstan has done me the honour to accept me as a husband in prospective."

"I suppose that, homely as it looks, this thing has some deadly story linked on to it—that it is the clue which will guide you in the solution of some mystery and the punishment of some crime."

"You are developing a certain unexpected vein of pawky humour, Watson, against which I must learn to guard myself."

"Good heavens! to think that you—you of all men— should be standing in my study. Well, you're not a spirit, anyhow."

He opened his eyes and gazed at the city before him—*his* city. His realm, his domain once… so long ago, it seemed. When he had left it ten years earlier, he had never intended to return—but here he was now, as glad as he had been a good *twenty* years ago to see it again.

Dear, dear old London. How he had missed her.

Half an hour later, he stepped onto British soil for the first time in nearly two years, and oh, how wonderful the feeling! To be standing on good, firm London ground once more… He stood there for a while, absorbing the vitality of the place and the beautiful sense of *coming home*.

He had dark business still to undertake, and his work in the end would not hold back the east wind. But he was home, and for the moment, that was all that mattered.

Sherlock Holmes was home at last.

Day 4: This Perfect Moment in Time

A low, insistent wail drifted from the direction of the cradle. Mary stifled a groan and sat up in bed, taking care not to rouse her husband.

Her caution was unnecessary. John pushed himself up as she was slipping out from underneath the bedclothes. "Go back to sleep, love," she murmured, trundling tiredly to the cradle.

He yawned. "As long as he's determined to be noisy, he'll keep me awake," he assured her.

She shook her head and bent down, lifting up the baby and wearily settling into the rocking chair to nurse him. However, Arthur did not seem to appreciate the feeding, and his cries became more pronounced. "John?" Mary said a trifle worriedly.

"He may be a bit colicky," John told her, slipping out of bed and shrugging on his dressing gown. "But it also may be nothing but restlessness. Let me have him."

She raised the baby up to John's waiting arms, and he hefted Arthur effortlessly to a more comfortable hold. "Now, now, my little man, you mustn't trouble your mother so. No, you mustn't."

Arthur continued to wail.

"I shall take him downstairs," John decided. "Get some sleep, Mary."

She wanted nothing more than to comply, but she knew she had to ask, "Are you certain?"

"Quite. Go on, back to bed."

She smiled wearily. "Yes, Doctor." She obediently climbed back into bed and gazed at him expectantly.

He smiled back at her, looking as tired as she felt. "Goodnight, darling."

"Goodnight, John…" Her farewell ended in a yawn, and she was back asleep nearly before he had left the room.

When she reawakened, it was still dark out, but her body's sense of time told her that it was time to rise. She turned on the gas, checked the little clock on the bedside table, and saw that it was five to seven. Throwing her dressing gown around her, she padded out of the bedroom and downstairs, halting at the door to the sitting room.

John sat in the rocker before a smouldering fire, asleep, hugging a peacefully sleeping Arthur to him. The baby's rosebud lips were slightly parted as his head rested upon his father's left shoulder. Mary winced a little at the thought of how much that shoulder would pain John once he woke up, but following that reaction, she wished fervently that she could have a photograph of this perfect moment in time. She hung in the doorway, studying the poignant tableau before her and committing every detail to memory, dimly lit though it was.

She noiselessly glided in and stretched herself out upon the settee, waiting for her family to awaken.

Day 5: Violinist on the Roof

I could not believe my eyes. In my many years of association with Mr. Sherlock Holmes, I have known and seen him perform some actions that were strange and even outside the boundaries of common sense. But never, in all the years I have known him, have I seen him do anything so completely *outré*.

"Good heavens! Holmes, what on earth are you—come down from there this instant before you fall and kill yourself!"

The Stradivarius paused only long enough for him to say, "My balance is perfect, my dear Watson. I shan't fall."

There are times when reasoning with Sherlock Holmes is like reasoning with a five-year-old: neither listens to you.

"For heaven's sakes, man, you're playing your violin on a *rooftop!*"

And so he was, perched upon the roof of the little country train station, looking for all the world like a great grey bird settled there. The violin paused again as he said simply, "I wanted to see if it was possible. I am pleased to say that the experiment is coming off splendidly."

"Until you finally lose your balance and *splendidly* come toppling to the ground!" I retorted heatedly.

Holmes ignored me, closing his eyes and throwing his soul into his music. The tune sounded like a folk dance, possibly of Jewish extraction—which puzzled me, since never before had I heard him perform any music that was not of European origin. Sherlock Holmes was quite content to cycle through several different styles of music for several hours. For the first half hour, I watched him anxiously; for the next half hour, I tried—and failed—to write out a case; and for the remaining three hours, I occupied my attention with a Clark Russell novel.

The sun hung low above the horizon when the last strains of music faded away. He slid down, as calmly as you please, from the ridgepole and let himself drop to hang on the eave—one-handed, his precious Stradivarius and bow in his left hand—for a moment before swinging and letting himself drop gracefully to the platform.

He flashed me a boyish grin, to which I responded with a raised eyebrow. "Satisfied?"

"Quite. That was most enjoyable. Shall we return to the inn now?"

Day 6: Mycroft's Gift

Young Mycroft Holmes tucked the lacy shawl under his arm and headed for the counter. A boy of twelve or thirteen was already there with a pair of shoes as he counted out his money, so Mycroft waited and let his mind drift.

Normally, Sherlock would be with him to buy his own gift for Mother, but this year, the boy had something different in mind. He'd told Mycroft that he intended to create a perfume for Mother with his chemicals, initiating an argument over the success of the venture. Mycroft had been privy to all twenty-three of his younger brother's malodorous failures since October and, incredibly enough, Sherlock's ultimate triumph.

He had to admit that it was quite a feat for a ten-year-old, even a *Holmes* ten-year-old.

His attention was pulled back to the present by the pleas of the boy in front of him. "Please, sir, it's Christmas…"

"I'm sorry, lad," said the clerk, "but you haven't got enough money."

Mycroft ran a swift analysis of the boy. Middle-class, of Scottish descent, buying a gift for his mother, and the mother was…

"But, sir, this my mother's last Christmas!"

The clerk shook his head. "I can't make exceptions, my boy. I'm sorry."

The boy looked utterly crushed. "Yes, sir," he murmured, pulling the shoes—dancing slippers—off the counter.

"Now wait a moment," Mycroft spoke up, laying a hand on the lad's arm. The younger boy looked up at him in surprise, and Mycroft met his gaze kindly. "How much more money do you need, young sir?"

Still surprised, the boy told him.

Without a moment's hesitation, Mycroft pulled out the correct amount out of his wallet and pressed into the boy's hand. "Take it."

The boy's hazel eyes widened. "Sir, I cannae let you do that!" he protested in an abruptly Scottish brogue.

"You need the money; now take it," Mycroft said firmly, with all the authority one had to develop to keep Sherlock Holmes under control. "Go on. Give your mother her gift with my compliments."

The hazel eyes misted over, and he didn't speak—or *couldn't* speak, more likely—for half a minute. At last: "God bless you, sir."

Mycroft left the shop feeling the solemnity of the season more profoundly than he had all month. The boy's gift had been a gift of love. Christmas itself marked the giving of the ultimate gift of love… a child…

When the young man returned home, not even young Sherlock could deduce why his older brother was so pensive.

XXX

Mycroft Holmes, with his eidetic memory, could not forget the Christmas of 1868, especially his mother's delighted surprise at Sherlock's homemade gift. But he did push it to the back of his mind to make room for more important things. Time passed, and he rose from governmental bookkeeper to *the* government itself. But one event in the summer '87, nearly two decades later, brought that particular Christmas back to full memory.

Sherlock was introducing his friend and roommate, Dr. John Watson, of whom Mycroft, of course, already knew a good deal. But he was struck with a sudden flash of recognition, and his mind worked speedily to identify the vaguely familiar face.

It was the eyes that did it. Those same warm, hazel eyes.

"I am glad to meet you, sir," said Mycroft, smiling and extending his hand. "I hear of Sherlock everywhere since you became his chronicler." He wouldn't introduce himself as the young man who'd given young John Watson the money he needed to buy his mother those dancing slippers. The Doctor obviously did not recognise him—Mycroft *had* gained quite a bit of weight since his youth—and Mycroft wouldn't dredge up possibly painful memories.

But he would tell Sherlock about it someday, meeting his brother's closest friend all those years ago on Christmas Eve…

Day 7: Wives of the Yard

"And they say that Christmas is a time of peace on earth," groused Annie Lestrade, sifting through the crate of decorations.

"It *is*, and *you* sound like my Tobias," Lisbeth Gregson grinned.

Annie favoured her friend with a scowl before turning to her business. Lisbeth merely shook her head and continued to untangle a string of dried berries.

Ellie Bradstreet entered the storage room, grimacing and holding her head. "Ach, but the chilluns are loud outside," she complained. "That lot could make a fine batch of constables, with lungs like that."

"I believe Sherlock Holmes beat you to the notion," Annie said absently. "Oh!" She rose from the crate and held up an angel. "She is lovely…"

"She's seen better days, darling," Ellie pointed out. "Perhaps you should retire her."

Annie shook her head. "If you think we should not use her, I would be willing to take her home with me. Rhiannon would love her."

"Take her, and my blessing," Ellie shrugged. "They're all of them *donated* decorations. Lizzie, how soon do you think we can decorate?"

"A few minutes, I should think."

"Splendid. Annie?"

"I'm ready right now, Ellie." Annie set the doll on a shelf and hefted up the crate.

Ellie sighed. "Ach, you're too small to be doing that, Ann. Let me help."

"You just take that crate over there," Annie directed, shifting her hold on her crate. "I'll be fine."

"If you say so..."

"I may be small, Eleanor Bradstreet, but I am not a weakling," Annie said firmly as she marched past her friend.

"I plead that living with a giant for a husband has skewed my view," Ellie called after her.

Annie considered that. "Skewed your view..."

"That's what I said."

"That was... strangely poetic, Ellie."

"Heaven help us. Annie, do *not* use that in one of your poems."

Annie flashed Ellie a completely unladylike grin. "A bit late for that, dear: it is already taking shape in my head."

Ellie glared back. "Hopeless romantic."

"You encourage me."

"I do not!"

"Ladies," Lisbeth's soft voice interjected. "Are we going to 'deck the hall,' or you going to stand there bickering? Remember, Annie—peace on earth."

Annie glared at her friend but set the crate down and drew a wreath from it. "Peace on earth," she repeated, scanning the walls for a place to hang the wreath. "I stand with Mr. Longfellow—there is no peace on earth, I say!" She flung the wreath out for dramatic emphasis before holding it up to a bare patch of wall.

Lisbeth merely raised an eyebrow.

"From the dregs of Whitechapel to the shores of our Indian possessions to our very own hearths," Annie continued firmly, eyeing the wall critically. "Now, I put to you that the angel was speaking of the same peace Christ spoke of at the Last Supper; therefore, I do not a-t'all appreciate the words 'peace on earth' bandied about at Christmastime when the Christian world is at its battiest."

Ellie stopped removing ornaments and clapped. "A teacher through and through, Annie, m'dear."

Annie carefully placed the wreath on the wall. "Forget it not, *neshomeleh*."

"As if I could ever!"

Lisbeth sighed. "I miss the other teacher of our little group."

Annie frowned. "As do I. Mary Watson certainly leaves a void in one's life when she's away."

"She could have stayed with one of us while the Doctor was away," said Ellie.

Annie shook her head. "John didn't want her in London right now." She sighed. "*Sherlock Holmes* leaves a void when he's not present, and that's the gospel truth!"

"I pray the men will find him soon," Ellie murmured.

Annie rounded on her, dark eyes widening. "Eleanor!"

"No, my Roger is not working on the case like your husbands are, but they *do* keep in touch!" Ellie snorted. "Do help with this garland, please."

Annie moved forward to help, and it was Lisbeth's turn to frown. "That information is confidential. Either Tobias and Geoffrey are speaking out of turn, or Roger *is* working on the case to some degree."

"Knowing Geoffrey, then, I'd say it's the latter," Ellie said firmly. "'Best of professionals,' and all that. Annie, your side of the garland is slipping."

Groaning, Annie adjusted it. "Thank you, Mr. Holmes, for that wonderful hon—I shouldn't say that." She bit her lip. "I don't even know if he is alive yet or not."

"He was kidnapped, Annie," Ellie reminded her gently, "not killed outright. Keep your chin up and keep praying."

Annie shook her head, stepping away from the garland. "It's been nearly a month now since he disappeared, Ellie. You know as well as I what can happen to a man in just *one week* if his kidnappers are ruthless enough. And, for all that radiant intellect… he is so very *fragile*. You have no *conception* of just how…" She nearly choked on the words as she looked down.

Ellie wrapped her arm around the smaller woman's shoulders. "Our lads will find him, love. They will. You just worry your head about your children, and leave the worrying of the investigation to the menfolk." She lifted Annie's chin to meet her gaze. "That's their job."

Annie released a shuddering breath. "But it *is* my job to worry after my family, and Sherlock Holmes is that." She let out a sound somewhere between a sob and a laugh. "Have you ever seen him with the children? Jeremy and Rhiannon long to be Irregulars, and, of course, Geoffrey will have none of it. But the *kinder* love Mr. Holmes that much, and he adores them in return—I know he does."

"He's quite a paradox, that one," Lisbeth observed as she inspected a nutcracker. "Acts like he's all brain, but he's all heart underneath—at least, I have it on good authority." She

24

nodded towards Annie. "'Fraid I haven't had much experience with the Great Detective myself; Tobias doesn't like him half so much as Geoffrey does, so…" She shrugged one shoulder.

"Who says Geoffrey *likes* Mr. Holmes?" said Ellie, hazel eyes twinkling.

"Well, he surely consults him often enough," Lisbeth returned.

Ellie cocked an eyebrow. "I once heard Geoffrey call the man… well, there were a few invectives involved."

Annie's eyes widened. "Ellie, are you saying that my husband *swore* in your presence?"

Ellie blushed slightly. "Not quite. I was at the Bow Street Station to see Roger, and I overheard them talking. It's really fascinating what you can hear when the lads don't know that you're about the place."

Annie and Lisbeth groaned. "You are *incorrigible*, Eleanor Alice Bradstreet," Annie retorted. "A-t'any rate, Geoffrey really does like Mr. Holmes very much, no matter what profanities he might level on the man. This kidnapping has certainly taken its toll on him; I sometimes have the impression that Geoffrey feels an almost fatherly duty towards Mr. Holmes."

Lisbeth blinked.

Ellie nodded sagely. "Roger has that impression, also."

Annie sighed and pressed her lips together. "Well, don't ever let Geoffrey know that. He'd first lecture us with all the authority of the Yard on how the exact opposite is true, and then he'd have to call upon the services of The Crooked Arrow to erase the memory of the entire conversation."

She shook her head. "My sister Gwynne wants me to join her temperance society, and I shan't deny that there's some valid logic in the notion of alcoholic abstinence. But how can I join in good conscience when I know that, quite often, the only way for Geoffrey to endure Mr. Holmes's... abrasive personality... is to drink it off at the Yarders' favourite haunt? I find that, upon hearing the 'horror tales,' I can't even blame him!"

"'A policeman's lot is not a happy one,'" Ellie sang as she hung up another wreath. She turned back to face her friends, hands on her hips. "Nor is the lot of a policeman's wife!"

"And *that's* the gospel truth," Lisbeth said firmly.

Day 8: A Season for Hope

He would never accept her, she knew. She had deceived him and hadn't possessed the moral courage to tell him the full truth before it was too late. She'd paid for it, too.

So when Sir Henry returned to Baskerville Hall two weeks before Christmas, she was not at all surprised that he made a round of seasonal calls without visiting Merripit House. Nor was she surprised that she received no invitation for the dinner to be hosted at the Hall on Christmas Eve.

It was a lonely *Navidad* she faced this year, as she had endured last year and would likely continue to endure for the rest of her life. She'd considered leaving Dartmoor many times, but where could she go? She had no close kin still alive in Costa Rica, nor had she ever had close friends there. And what would she do if she left? Teaching was the only thing she *could* do and the prospect did not appeal to her. With frugality, she could keep herself comfortable at Merripit House with the money she had.

She did not want to stay in Dartmoor, but she could not bring herself to leave.

These thoughts were racing through her mind for the umpteenth time when she heard a knock on the door. Odd enough that it was late in the evening, but on *Christmas Eve*, no less?

But if the knock was startling, the visitor was even more so. He was thinner than she recalled, paler... but at the same time more erect, nobler even than before. His face creased into an uncertain smile as she opened the door.

"Sir Henry," she breathed.

"Miss St—Mrs.—erm, Miss Beryl?" His smile grew lopsided with embarrassment. "Ah, Merry Christmas. May I come in?"

"Certainly," her lips replied for her while she tried to fathom exactly why the baronet would be calling upon her *now* and on Christmas Eve, of all nights, while he was hosting a dinner. Her heartbeat quickened fractionally at the warmth in his large blue eyes.

He cast a reminiscing gaze about the sitting room as she led in him into it. "This place has hardly changed." He turned to her with a fond look that somehow managed to look more affectionate than a smile. "Neither have you."

"I hope that is not so," she said quietly.

He looked down and cleared his throat. "Yes, well, I'm terribly sorry I haven't called upon you sooner. It has been a busy two weeks..."

"Yes, I know. Haven't you a dinner to be hosting?" She froze, startled at the bitterness in her voice. Why had she lashed out at him like that, of all people?

"I do," he murmured. "I did purposefully leave you out of my invitations, Miss Beryl."

She frowned, more curious than affronted. "Yes?"

"I wished our first meeting to be more private. I've a question to ask you, if I may."

Surely he must have heard her heart pounding! "Please do."

Slowly, tenderly, he took her hand in his. "Then let me be plain about it," he said quietly. "There was once a connexion between us. Whatever else was wrong with our world, the fact is that I loved you and that I love you still."

She stared at him; her heart leapt for joy at what her mind told her could not be true.

"I love you, Beryl," he repeated, his honest face as earnest as she'd ever seen it. "I love you."

She shook her head and stepped back. "I wronged you. I knew... I *knew* what my husband intended for you, and, God forgive me, I was too selfish."

"You were afraid," he protested.

"My fear was selfish," she said firmly, removing her hand from his. "If I had truly loved you, I would have warned you sooner and more fully. I should have told you all."

"Then you *did* love me."

"Sir Henry, please." Why did he have to make this difficult for her? She had no right to be in his life, not when she'd endangered it by her silence.

She wanted him as much as he wanted her, but it would not be right.

"I forgive you, Beryl," he said gently. "What is it that the Bible says? Love keeps no record of wrongdoings? Beryl, I keep no record of yours."

"Then you have a purer heart than I," she murmured as she looked down, unable to hold his intense gaze.

"I see. You cannot forgive yourself." He sighed. "Very well, then. I can wait for you to be able to forgive yourself. And I warn you, I can be a very patient man."

She felt colour rise to her cheeks.

He bent over her hand and kissed it. "May you have a fine Christmas, Miss Beryl."

"And you." She meant it with all her heart.

She risked a glance up and saw him grin. "Thank you. Never mind, I can see myself out." He nodded respectfully and, half a minute later, she heard the front door open and close. She sank onto the settee, sobs hitching in her throat. She was unsure why she cried—joy, despair, self-recrimination, and hope vied for dominance.

But when she awoke the next morning, it was the first time in a very long time that she looked forward to the new day.

She allowed herself to hope that, someday, she would be able to forgive herself.

Day 9: Highly Inconvenient

"Watson…"

"Do not even *consider* it, Holmes."

"But…"

"No."

"I could merely—"

"*No.*"

"You *must* be experiencing the same difficulty! It is entirely impossible that you should not!"

"I absolutely refuse to drink the blood of another human being, no matter how bloody powerful the urge becomes!"

"…mayn't I simply feed on a criminal?"

"*No*, Holmes."

"Not even an *important* criminal?"

"Oh, for heaven's sake…"

"Moriarty! Couldn't I go feed on him? …Watson? Watson, why are you knocking your head against your desk?"

"Sherlock Holmes! Consider what you are *saying*! Are you telling me that you want to drink the *blood of Professor James Moriarty?*"

"Ohhh. On second thought, no, I don't believe so."

"Thank goodness for that!"

"But I am *hungry*, Watson!"

"Ohhh, for heaven's… *Blast* that idiot vampire for thinking it amusing to convert us."

"There must be *some* way out of this…"

"Perhaps we should tell Mycroft."

"WHAT? No! Watson, are you daft, man? I'd never hear the end of it!"

"Very well. Perhaps we *should* go to the Professor—he might have an idea or two…"

"Capital. Let's go."

"…I beg your pardon?"

"My dear Watson, I would much rather go crawling in on my hands and knees to my arch-nemesis than face *my brother* with my newfound vampirism. You have quite obviously never seen Mycroft enraged."

"Oh, Holmes, *really*."

"Watson. Vampires, werewolves, and criminal masterminds have *absolutely nothing* upon a furious Mycroft Tristan Holmes. Shall we go?"

"May the good Lord give me strength…"

Day 10: Stepping through the Wardrobe

At the tender age of nine, Sherlock Edward Holmes was recognised by kith and kin alike as a genius.

He had already mastered the violin and could probably have become another Mozart had he so chosen. But his considerable powers of memory, intuition, intellect, and the five senses were applied to a wide range of interests, including chemistry, linguistics, visual art, and horsemanship. He was the joy and terror of every mere mortal that attempted to teach him, and he was the envy of his peers, including his cousins.

Ethel Holmes, two years Sherlock's junior, was no exception.

Sherlock and Ethel did not get on very well. Ethel was jealous and catty in her spite, and Sherlock retorted by being insufferable in his prodigy brilliance. Things came to a head in that summer, the summer of 1867, when Ethel and her elder sister, Marianne, came to stay at the Holmes estate with their recently widowed mother, who had fallen quite ill in her grief.

Sherlock was rather less than thrilled at the invasion of Rosewood Hall.

"It isn't fair!" he complained to his brother. "Ethel is such a brat, and Mother insists that I should feel *sorry* for her!"

Sixteen-year-old Mycroft set aside *The Pickwick Papers* with a sigh. "And so you should, Sherlock. Do you remember Mother's illness after the baby died?"

Sherlock's stomach twisted. He well remembered those terrible days, two years earlier, when their baby sister had been stillborn and Mother had fallen deathly ill. "That was different," he muttered.

"How so?" Mycroft said quietly, his near-white eyes unsettling in their intensity.

Sherlock fidgeted and looked down, unable to hold his brother's gaze. The little boy could hold his own against children, youths, and adults alike, regardless of class or education, but he had never yet won out over his elder brother. If Sherlock's intellect was immense, Mycroft's was immeasurable, and they both knew it.

After a minute, Sherlock spoke again, his voice subdued. "She *is* hateful, brother mine."

Mycroft's expression had softened. "I know, little one, and for that also she deserves your pity. Ethel has never liked you, it is true, but she has been exceedingly bitter since Uncle Aethelstan's death. Father may not often be home, Sherlock, but at least we still have him."

XXX

Sherlock held no quarrel with the pretty, fourteen-year-old Marianne, even if there was no great love between them. She

36

thought him a funny and occasionally sweet boy; he thought her a nice, if insipid, girl. At least, they could interact civilly, and even affectionately.

So Marianne would sometimes go so far as to help Sherlock avoid her sister. Sherlock would break into a run for the less-inhabited parts of the vast, pre-Georgian manor. In this way, he came to explore his own home as he never had before, searching out the darkest, dustiest nooks and crevices. He refused to let himself hope for something as fantastic as hidden treasure, but he felt that he must find something *worth* finding sooner or later.

It was on one such run-from-Ethel-turned-expedition that he found It. It stood draped in a sheet at the far end of the room, and the only other thing in the room was a bluebottle on the windowsill that spun for a moment before going still. Sherlock approached the far end of the room with slow, measured steps as if treading on sacred ground.

As he tugged at the sheet, it rippled down like a gentle waterfall.

It was a wardrobe. An exquisitely carved, mahogany-hued wardrobe. Sherlock thought he had never seen anything so lovely or so mysterious in his life.

He reached out a tentative hand and opened the right-hand door, which swung open to reveal a row of fur coats. Why... why would his parents keep such a work of art in a spare room, merely for storing coats? Surely, something must be hidden in the *back* of it.

He stepped inside and brushed through the fur, reaching for the back of the wardrobe. But it didn't come. Frowning, he made his way deeper in, hand extended...

And felt sharp pricks against his palm. He jumped back, paused, pressed forward. Grey light broke through the fur, and then he came out on the other side.

Into a snowy wood.

It was summertime right now, and yet he had walked right through the wardrobe as one would a door... and it was snowing on the other side. Not only that, but these were not the woods of the Holmes estate. Whereas Rosewood possessed mostly leafy trees, the majority of *these* trees were clearly evergreen.

And it was *snowing*.

Sherlock took one step out onto the white ground before stopping and gazing up at the silver sky. He turned to look over his shoulder, saw the spare room beyond the proper door of the wardrobe. Mycroft would have stopped right there, turned fully 'round, gone back. Mycroft would have approached the thing with detached, scientific interest.

Sherlock was not Mycroft.

He stepped fully out into the wintry landscape. A delighted grin spread across his small face—it was *lovely* here. He cupped his bare hands together and watched as one detailed snowflake after another landed on his tanned skin and seeped into it. He scarcely noticed the cold, so *alive* did he feel.

He broke into a run on the path that seemed to lead from the wardrobe. The snow was powdery and flew each time his feet pounded against the earth. He laughed for the sheer joy of it all. Then he saw something which truly made his breath catch.

His wandering gaze caught the roots first. They looked like a tree's roots, but they were unmistakably *iron*. His eyes were drawn upward, along the stem that was unquestionably the stem of a lamppost, 'til they reach the gas lamp atop the... stem, trunk, pole? As mad as he knew it sounded, it was a lamppost grown from the ground. He had no idea how such a thing could be, but he could not deny the reality his eyes saw.

Inexplicably, the sight was welcoming, calming, comforting. The flame burned bright, a warm glow in a beautiful but cold forest.

Sherlock could not begin to fathom where he was. His first supposition was somewhere on the Continent—the place reminded him of photographs he'd seen—but how on earth could he have crossed over from England to the Continent in such a fashion? He might as well have been transported to another world.

And that truly set his mind working. What if he *had* been transported to another world? What if magic *did* exist, despite Mycroft's arguments to the contrary? And why would *he*,

Sherlock Edward Holmes, be sent to another world, and how, how, *how?*

He pressed his fingertips to his lips in contemplation as he leaned against the lamppost. It was the matter of a few seconds. He wanted to explore this fascinating new land, whatever it was and whatever happened to him for it. He smiled as he recalled a line from Shakespeare.

The game's afoot!

Day 11: Not a Stranger

The twelve-year-old halted and stared at his friend. "Breandán, it's a graveyard."

"I can see that, Sherlock."

"It's a *graveyard*, Brean."

"Is there something wrong with eating lunch in a graveyard?"

Sherlock continued to stare at the gypsy boy. "Graveyards, by definition, Brean, are yards—to whit, open green spaces—full of *graves*, which inter *dead people*."

Breandán Delaney's emerald-green eyes blinked placidly. "Aye. Now, are we going to eat?"

"But—but…" For one of the few times in his young life, Sherlock Edward Holmes was struck nearly speechless.

"Ach, I forgot—you English think it's disrespectful. Lor' A'mighty, Sherlock, when my clan reaches London, we *live* in our old graveyard for a week while we clean the whole lot up."

Sherlock's eyes went round. "But…"

A mischievous and very Gaelic fire lit in the green eyes. "Ah, I see how it is. You're a-feared to be in the graveyard, aren't you?"

Sherlock felt his face flush. "I am not!"

"Well, then…" The Irish boy gestured him forward with a flourish.

"Fool Tinkers," the English boy muttered as he stomped after his friend. In spite of himself, his gaze roamed the tombstones, taking in everything. Even when he was irritated, his brain simply did not *stop*, and, sometimes, that was a bit difficult to live with. "I think some of my people are buried here," he said in a tone respectful to the dead but loud enough for Breandán to hear.

"I thought they were all't that private cemetery at Rosewood Hall."

Sherlock pointed to a grave marker that read simply: *Emily Love, October 19th, 1817—March 30th, 1819.* "I believe I recall hearing the name *Love* somewhere in the family genealogy."

"Ah."

"…she died so young."

"That happens, Sherlock," Breandán said gently.

Sherlock shook himself out of his slightly mournful thoughts. "I am sorry, Breandán—I was not thinking about—"

Breandán shook his head. "It *happens*, Sherlock. Tears can't bring them back." He sounded as if he was trying to convince himself.

Sherlock could not help but thinking of his sister, the baby that had been stillborn when he was little. "No... but I think... I think it's not a *bad* thing to cry. Not always. I think that... I think that we need to be *able* to cry." He glanced up at Breandán, who frowned contemplatively. "Do you understand what I am saying?"

"I think so," Breandán nodded. "I think I do." Silence fell over them, not at all awkward or even sad. "Well," the Irish boy said at last, "we'd best eat up. Don't forget I've got t' be with m'da this afternoon."

"Of course." Sherlock took one last look at the marker of the baby girl—was she a distant cousin or was she no relation at all?—before joining Breandán on the warm grass. Oddly, he no longer felt a sense of trespass, but one of... acceptance.

These were his people, by ties of blood or land, and he was theirs.

Day 12: The Gift

Holmes watched as Watson turned the pieces over in his gloved palm, his eyes brown and sad in the November murk. "It is not salvageable?" Holmes ventured tentatively.

Watson sighed. "It is, but it would be less expensive—and more practical—simply to buy a new revolver. This is nearly two decades old, after all." He paused.

"But?" Holmes prompted gently.

The Doctor shook his head. "With first the move and the wedding and now the baby on the way... I simply can't afford it right now." His military posture drooped marginally, but very few things made John Hamish Watson droop that much.

Holmes understood his friend's sorrow—Watson's Adams had been an extension of his hand for over nineteen years. It had seen as much service as any army revolver still in service of Queen and country, and the irony of it was that it had probably seen more—Watson's particular Adams had been replaced in the army years ago.

"Here." Holmes passed his own revolver to his friend, flashing him a quicksilver smile. "You can use this at present— you know you shall use it more than I."

Watson accepted the gun with an exasperated smile. "Yeees, well..." He cleared his throat. "Thanks, old fellow."

Holmes twitched in his seat as Watson reached under the tree for the last present and tore open the wrapping. Eileen Watson caught Holmes's fidgeting and visibly suppressed a smile, then turned back to her husband as his breath caught. "Oh, *Holmes…*"

"It is the correct make?" Holmes said anxiously, taking in Watson's stunned expression. "I was not quite certain…"

Watson shook his head, smiling that smile that said he was close to tears and laughter both. "It is perfect, Holmes, truly." He lifted the revolver and peered at the inscription, a simple *S.E.H. to J.H.W., Christmas 1899.* "My dear fellow—" his voice was thick, and when he raised his head, his eyes were glistening— "*thank you.*"

Holmes squirmed slightly. He and Watson had been exchanging gifts for many years, and he had not yet grown accustomed to all the emotion that could sometimes be involved. "You are most welcome, my good Watson." He caught Eileen's twinkling green gaze and took encouragement from it—John Watson really was a fortunate man to have gotten a second match made in heaven. "After all, I can't have my bodyguard forever without his own weapon, can I?"

Eileen laughed, and Watson shook his head, his broad shoulders shaking. "No, I don't suppose you can."

Holmes settled back into his chair and sighed in contentment, equilibrium restored. "Merry Christmas, Watson."

"Merry Christmas, Holmes."

Day 13: WANTED: A Friend

WANTED:

Lodger to split rent for comfortable, middle-class flat. Male, please, preferably twenties or thirties. Must be of quiet habits and sturdy, reliable disposition, not easily alarmed by potentially disastrous happenings. Apply to Mr. S. Holmes at 58 Montague St.

He put down the old newspaper with a grin. "Potentially disastrous happenings," indeed—they'd had no end of those ever since that first case a year ago. Good lord, had it been only a year?

It felt as if they'd been sharing rooms together forever, and that was by no means an unpleasant sensation. He could not imagine his life without the remarkable man he felt privileged to call "friend." His grin faded as he wondered if he truly met the criteria Holmes had in mind when they'd met.

"Watson, why are you standing around?" Holmes cried sing-song as he whirled into the sitting room just then. "There is a performance of Tchaikovsky at the Royal Albert Hall tonight, and, by George, we shall not miss it!"

Watson set the paper down on the desk and smiled at his friend's infectious enthusiasm. "Very well, then, Holmes."

"By the pensive expression I observed upon your face as I entered, I deduce that whatever has you down is in the text of that yellowed specimen of the press, my boy," Holmes said cheerily. "Come now, what is it?"

Caught now, Watson handed the paper with its circled content over to the younger man. "I found it when I was organising the papers you so kindly left strewn about the sitting room," he said pointedly. As usual, all arrows bounced off the armour that was Sherlock Holmes's indifference to anything and everything that did not fall under the category of "current most important priority."

Holmes's grin widened, and he laughed. "So much for that, eh?" he said, referencing the advertisement rather than his earlier mess. "I did not receive a single application until Stamford introduced us."

"Fortunately for me." Watson could not fathom the tinge of bitterness his voice held.

Holmes's eyebrows drew together. "Fortunately for us both," he corrected. "Watson, do you... do you think me not fully satisfied with you as a fellow lodger?"

There was nothing for it now: he had to reveal his insecurities whether he liked it or not. "Well, I would not quite say that I have 'quiet habits'... or a quiet temper, for that matter."

Holmes threw down the paper with an exasperated huff. "My dear fellow, I do *not* make such decisions as a choice in flat mates lightly. I was perfectly satisfied to go halves with you, and I remain satisfied. You must think very little of me, indeed, to think for one moment that a slight upon your character would not reflect upon me."

Watson watched him in astonishment. Sherlock Holmes was not an easy man to befriend, by all accounts, and yet Watson had never had much difficulty in getting past the barriers Holmes had erected—to the shock of many good men down at Scotland Yard. But to hear from Holmes's own lips that he not only enjoyed but *valued* their friendship… was nothing short of a revelation.

"I… I don't know what to say," Watson admitted.

Holmes gave him a look one might give to a particularly dense brother. Watson did not know why that term entered his mind, but it did.

"Say that you'll come with me tonight and leave behind forever this nonsense of being anything less than the perfect companion. Really, Watson, you do underrate yourself deplorably sometimes!"

Day 14: Bereft

The end of the world is cold.

The icy air penetrates your clothing, your skin, and cuts straight to the bone. You are never completely warm.

Your head throbs, less from the cold and more from the pitiless starkness surrounding you. The sunlight is intense and harsh. The blue of the sky burns into your eyes as much as does the white of the snow. If icicles were driven directly into your skull, they could inflict no greater torment than the brilliant, unforgiving day of Tibet.

Living from day to day is a never-ending exercise in endurance. You wonder how much further you can go before you simply… break.

You've broken before, or at least come near it. You've burned and bled and screamed 'til your throat went raw and your voice silent, and still you screamed. You've experienced terrors that belong to a darker, more savage time, and they live on in your dreams.

But that isn't the worst.

The worst is reliving the hour that you made the decision to *leave*. The worst is reliving *his* cries, watching him and longing to go down to him and comfort him…

And, even in your dreams, you don't do it right. You didn't then, and you don't now.

You don't go down, you don't tell him that it's all right, all's well, you're not dead… You stay there on that ledge, *watching* him.

You're not a brain without a heart, whatever people might think, but… in just that one moment, you *might* have been.

You're exhausted. You're tired of pain, tired of falling prey to sickness and depression, tired of cold, tired of living a lie, tired of running, tired of criminals and madmen, and you want it to *stop. All* of it.

You want to go home. You want your warm hearth, your bullet-scarred wall, your chemical-stained deal table, your comfortable armchair, your full pipe rack… You want your dearest friend, want to beg him for forgiveness, want to see the baby boy that's just been born to him…

You want to go home. You want so terribly to go home.

The sun falls below the Himalayan peaks, and dusk settles upon the end of the world, bringing relief to your tortured eyes. The first stars appear in the darkling sky, one by one—and one point of light shines brighter than the rest, deep in the eastern sky. For the first time since receiving that telegram from your brother, you smile. Just a small, weary smile, but, in this moment, you feel lighter of heart.

Behold, good tidings of great joy, which shall be to all people.

Merry Christmas, my dear Watson.

Day 15: A Policeman's Lot

Is not at all a happy one. Gilbert and Sullivan were bloody right about that.

Professional to the all-too-literal end, Lestrade did not slam the door shut as he entered his office, but he came close. Quite close. Gritting his teeth, he stomped over to the desk and started removing his personal effects, which were thankfully few.

At first, he had been in shock after being apprised of his dismissal by the Chief Inspector. After all, he had been in the Met for twenty years—who *wouldn't* be left reeling from news like that? All because of a viscount's fool son. The upper class was a plague upon the hardworking constables and detectives alike of the London Metropolitan.

But then, as the news circulated with ruthless speed through the Yard, he had caught Gregson's mixed expression of pity and relief. Yes, the very Saxon Gregson no longer had to worry that the apparently Gallic Lestrade would contest for further promotion. Lestrade woke from his shock to a righteous fury and, ignoring Bradstreet's genuine dismay (*"Geoff, please, let me talk with the Old Man"*), set off for his office with a speed that could have rivalled Sherlock Holmes's on a case, despite the little detective's bad foot.

Now, however… now, he slumped into his chair, his anger having expended itself and leaving him with no support to keep him upright. He cupped his chin in his hand and sighed. He didn't know where he'd go from here: like so many of his companions, the Yard was all he'd ever known. And yet he had to find work *somewhere*… Annie was heavily with child once again. Not to mention the fact that her language tuition was meant to support *his* income, not to support the family itself.

He could not begin to fathom how he'd explain this to her.

His mind wandered back to the case and, inevitably, to his amateur colleague. Sherlock Holmes had supplemented his investigation every step of the way, and he was every bit as convinced of the Honourable David Fitzwilliam's guilt as Lestrade was. (An agreement betwixt him and Holmes? Great Scott, miracles *did* happen.) Lestrade had arrested Fitzwilliam, fully aware that he was treading on thin ice.

Fitzwilliam's father had intervened.

Lestrade's career at the Yard was finished.

He rubbed at the headache forming behind his eyes—stress-induced, certainly—and sighed again. Well, he'd best complete his packing and make certain his cases and files were distributed properly—

"*Geoffrey Michael Lestrade!*"

Lestrade was on his feet in an instant, watching wide-eyed as Roger Bradstreet burst through the door. "*Merciful heavens*, man, what is wrong with you?"

"You little son of a moon curser—*you're not being dismissed!*"

"*What?*"

Bradstreet gulped for breath before pressing on. "Holmes! It was all his bloody doing! He argued something fierce with the Old Man and threatened to *unleash his bloody Whitehall brother* on Mitchell if he let you go!"

Lestrade dropped into his chair again, the world pulled out from beneath his feet for the second time in one afternoon. "You jest," he said faintly.

"I bloody well don't!" Bradstreet boomed. "Go see Holmes for yourself!" Without waiting for Lestrade to reply, the larger man hauled his smaller friend out of his seat by the arm and propelled him out the door.

Dr. Watson was running up to them in the hall, wearing the biggest grin Lestrade had ever seen on the young veteran's face. "Inspector! I see Bradstreet told you the news!"

Lestrade felt the colour drain from his cheeks. "He didn't."

"He jolly well did!" Watson retorted happily. "Called down the wrath of God on your Chief Inspector—I don't think that I have ever seen Holmes more eloquent or more furious."

Lestrade's eyebrows hit his hairline. "I've seen him as both at once, and it is rather... unforgettable."

Watson laughed outright and clapped him on the shoulder. "Go back to your superior, Lestrade. I think you'll find him eating a large dish of humble pie, served up *à la Sherlock Holmes*."

"I should like to speak with Mr. Holmes first."

Watson's smile turned contemplative. "He left immediately for Baker Street, Lestrade. I rather think…" The Doctor left the sentence unfinished, but Lestrade could complete it in his head: *Holmes did not want gratitude*. The little detective had known the young madman longer than Watson had—he knew well how adverse Holmes was to the slightest display of thanks.

He nodded and smiled slowly at Watson. "Very well, then. Give him my thanks for me?"

Watson smiled back in understanding—sentiments that Holmes could not endure from other people, he could endure from his flat mate. "Of course. Good day to you, Lestrade, Bradstreet."

"Good day, Doctor!"

"Good day, Doctor, and thank you."

Lestrade waited until Watson's broad shoulders had disappeared in the flow of indoor traffic. Then he turned, straightened his shoulders, and set off for the Chief Inspector's office.

Day 16: Guardian Angel

She did not *walk* so much as she *flitted* from lighted window to lamppost to lighted window. No lamp could pierce far into a London Particular, but she took what help she could get. Jemima had begged her to stay the night, but Mary wanted— needed—to get home.

For Jemima's sake, she could *visit* Whitechapel, but she drew the line at staying the night.

She picked up her old skirts as she trod through a small stream on the kerb, forcing herself not to think about *what* she was stepping in. Whenever she came here to visit her old friend, she wore old, ragged clothes so as to blend in with the inhabitants of London's most notorious district. Were she to wear clothes marking her out as a member of the middle class, she had no doubt that she would be assaulted, whether for her money or for other things.

XXX

John sighed as he clasped his Gladstone closed and turned to bid his patient farewell. There wasn't a blessed thing to be seen out the window. He loathed Particulars—the damp chill seeped past cloth and skin and settled into the damaged bones in his left shoulder and right thigh. From a purely practical standpoint, London was a foolish place for an injured war veteran to make a home, and yet, after seven years, he could not dream of leaving.

He opened the door and stepped out into the atmospheric pea soup.

XXX

Mary heard footsteps behind her for a mere four seconds before she was pulled back by her arm. She screamed and whirled on her attacker, her free hand reaching for the derringer John insisted she carry on her at all times. The man—he was a man, but she could tell nothing beyond that—reached for her left arm as he twisted her right one. Screaming again (*dear God in heaven, let someone hear!*), she tried to aim the gun at the man.

His hand wrapped around her left wrist, and they struggled for the derringer. Mary squeezed the trigger.

The little bullet went wide and might have struck a lamppost—she couldn't be sure. His hand constricted around her wrist, and she cried out in pain. He pulled her to him with her captive arm and, irresistibly, twisted her left arm around behind her to join the other. She screamed again as she was jerked back against him, the pain in her arms white-hot and blinding and leaving her unable to struggle.

"Now, now, my pretty," her attacker whispered in her ear. "Just you relax now."

She whimpered in pain, hot tears rolling down her face.

"Ah, you are a spirited one, aren't you? Just relax, and this shall be quick."

He began to drag her away, and she found she could toss in his grip. "No! No! No! No…" But he was much stronger, and she soon felt the cold iron of a lamppost against her back as her arms were pulled around it.

"Shh, shh." She could just make out the glint of the man's teeth, feeling rather than seeing his grin as he bound her forearms roughly to the post. "I'm not worried about being overheard, mind you, thanks to this rum fog, but I don't see the sense in putting up a fuss."

"Let me go!" Mary half-screamed, half-sobbed, jerking away from her captor. "Let me go!"

"Shh, dearie, shh. None of that, now, or I shall have to be rough with you, see?"

Her arms bound securely to the post, he sidled around in front of her and put his hands on his hips, whistling in surprise. "Well, now, seems I caught me a lady." She caught the flash of his teeth again. "And here I thought I was getting me a dollymop."

"Don't, please, don't," Mary pleaded. "I can give you money—anything. Just please don't—"

But her pleas were muffled by lips forcefully covering her own, eliciting whimpers deep in her throat. Then his body was pressed up against hers once more, sending thrills of terror through her. She writhed beneath him, but he pressed her tightly against the lamppost, his lips still locked around hers and his hands busy with her clothes.

Father in Heaven, if ever You loved me, help me now!

XXX

John was trudging a bit less than gamely through the fog when he heard a wail that stopped him and chilled him to the bone. He knew that kind of wail. Then the woman—for female the voice was—screamed.

He took off running, adrenaline compensating for the debilitating ache spreading through his bad leg. He drew his revolver as the woman screamed again, and he would have sworn the voice sounded familiar. *Please, dear Lord, let me arrive on time.*

He ran straight into someone, bowling them over. The person swore and shoved him away, and John just noticed that the person, a man, was only half-clothed. He took only a split-second to see that, because his gaze was immediately drawn to the figure sagging against a lamppost, bound and even less clothed than the man, blouse, jacket, and skirt hanging in rags about her.

She looked up, and her expression of terror changed instantly to one of shocked relief. "*John!*"

Good heavens… "*Mary.*"

With a snarl, the man at his feet leapt up and tackled him. Mary screamed again. Broader than his assailant, John stumbled but stood his ground, attempting to bring his Adams to bear. Metal gleamed dully in the lamplight, and John saw white as his bad shoulder erupted in a blaze of agony.

"JOHN!"

He squeezed the trigger, the shot shattering the air around them. The other man howled and staggered back towards Mary, the metal gleaming again. Desperate fury driving him, John leapt at the other man. Mary screamed again as they fell into the road.

They struggled for the gun, and John felt the other's finger tighten around the trigger. The revolver went off, knocking them both down again, but the shot went wide, mercifully missing not only John but Mary as well. Then the man was struggling just to get out of John's grip. Both men were strong, but both were hurt, and John felt the man break free. He staggered after the man, but he was gone, vanished into the fog that had disgorged him.

Panting, John turned to Mary… And fervently wished that he could have killed that… that monster…

A scarlet line ran from Mary's right collarbone down her upper arm. John's rugby tackle must have knocked the knife off-course, keeping it from slashing across her throat.

The Ripper.

"Mary," he pushed out in a croak as he returned to her and fished out his knife to cut her loose.

"John!" she sobbed. "Oh, thank God you were here!"

"Shh, Mary, you are going to be all right," he soothed as he worked at the ropes. "Why on earth were you here, and dressed like this?"

"F-friend," Mary choked out. "Lives here. C-clothes to k-keep me from b-being a t-target…"

John understood that much, but why the *devil* was she out *alone* in Whitechapel at night in the middle of a Particular? "Mary, haven't you been reading the papers? The stories about the Ripper? That he targets prostitutes in Whitechapel?" He didn't mean to sound harsh, but the aftershock and the horror of the thing put an edge in his voice sharp enough to cut a person on.

"D-didn't th-think…" She broke down completely, and John could not fault her at all for it. He shuddered convulsively to think of what *would* have happened had he not arrived in time.

The newspapers would have had another sensational episode to report, Scotland Yard another murder on their hands, and the Ripper another tally to his bloody score. Mrs. Forrester would lost a daughter, the Forrester children not so much a governess as an older sister, and John the only woman he had ever really loved.

A terrible little part of his mind wondered if Holmes would have even cared.

Of course, he would not have cared, a nasty voice hissed.

He bloody well would *have, John Hamish Watson,* retorted another voice, *and he would have because he cares about* you, *no matter the depths to which he sinks.*

The last of the rope fell away, allowing Mary to sink gratefully into his embrace. "Oh, John," she sobbed.

He wrapped her shawl around her partially exposed torso before lifting carefully her into his arms, mindful of his injured shoulder. It screamed in protest, but he ignored it, taking one step forward, then another. He knew he could ignore it only for so long—they had to get to a better part of town, and quickly.

XXX

Mary felt as if she was drowning in shame. She was ashamed of her foolishness, ashamed that her fiancé must see her exposed, ashamed that he had to rescue her at all, ashamed that she could not stop herself from sobbing like a little girl. And yet...

And yet she saw the grim determination in John's tense features, and she suddenly felt as if she was in the presence of a guardian angel.

XXX

It was late in the morning when at last Watson returned home from his work in Whitechapel. Holmes had a greeting poised upon his lips when Watson staggered through the sitting room door, clothes torn, mudded, and blood-soaked, the stain radiating from his bad shoulder. "My dear Watson!" Holmes cried, leaping to his feet from the settee.

Watson looked up from returning his revolver to his desk, fatigue, residual anger, and pain dimming his hazel eyes and turning them cognac brown. "Holmes," he began, his voice as dull as his eyes. "I beg you not to deduce what has happened."

"Watson, you are asking the impossible," Holmes murmured. *You have been in a fight in Whitechapel—I know that mud—and you were not the only injured party. You smell of disinfectant— there was a victim; you were defending them. That jagged hole in your clothes was clearly made by a knife.*

Even Lestrade could have put the clues together, though Holmes did not dare to do so aloud.

"Holmes. Please." Those expressive eyes were certainly a force to be reckoned with; Holmes merely sighed and shook his head.

"At least tell me that you've had the shoulder tended to."

"Yes." The relief in Watson's voice was profound.

"Very well, old man." Holmes forced levity into his tone, for the doctor's sake. "I do hope that you plan on going to bed soon; you look dreadful."

Watson shook his head in turn and shot Holmes a grateful smile before leaving the room. Holmes frowned contemplatively and turned to retrieve his cherrywood from the pipe rack. Scotland Yard had not yet approached him regarding the Ripper Case—Lestrade and Gregson, despite multiple protests, were not allowed to investigate, either. The powers that be apparently deemed Inspectors Abberline, Moore, and Andrews to be enough the handle the case. Ha. Their incompetence was not even amusing. But…

But Watson had now been dragged into this sordid affair.

And not only dragged, but stabbed, right in the shoulder that had cast him out of the army in the first place.

Holmes puffed furiously at his pipe, his hand clenching around the bowl. Whatever this monster called himself—Saucy Jack, Jack the Ripper—he would not continue his reign of terror for long. He was about to find out just how very great a mistake it was to injure the man Sherlock Holmes called "friend."

Day 17: The Actor

"Come along, Ed, and quit gawking at Irving."

Sherlock did not deign to glance at his associate as he whispered back, "In a moment. I want to watch to the end of the scene."

"Very well. Just don't get The Governor riled when he's done, there's a good chap?"

Sherlock nodded irritably and kept his gaze focused upon Henry Irving, manager and star of the Lyceum Theatre, currently rehearsing for the next production. Irving was a brilliant actor—it was easy to see why people flocked to his performances. Sherlock had come here himself as a member of the audience before...

Before.

Now he was investigating a murder that had occurred just outside the theatre two weeks ago, and, to do so, he had gone undercover as a young actor named Edward Love. Just now, he really *should* be looking into one of the other actors, but the artist in him had been held captive by Irving's rehearsal. He played Shylock magnificently, imbuing him with a dignity seldom found in performances of the character.

"The Merchant of Venice *is one of my favourite Shakespeare plays. I have always liked Portia very much—her devotion, her intelligence, her wit…*"

"*Very much like you.*"

"*Sherlock Edward Holmes, have you no shame?*"

"*You know I haven't.*"

He shut his eyes against the unwelcome memory, pushed it to the back of his mind. Annie Middleton had been dead for a year now, but memories of her still had the maddening ability to distract him from his work. Sighing, his hand rose to his chest to clutch at an all-too-physical ache.

He still missed her, terribly.

As he remained in his seat, watching Irving deliver his lines, Sherlock could not help but wonder who was the better actor: the man who could bring crowds night after night to a performance, or a man who could convince the world day by day that he was not dying on the inside of heartache?

Day 18: Long Time Falling

All his life, he was flying.

From birth, he was destined for great heights. He spoke articulately from an early age, read, wrote, scribbled out mathematical equations far beyond the average understanding for his age. He rose.

He completed school astonishingly early, entered university immediately afterwards, stayed on for years until he reached his doctorate, only in his twenties. He gained recognition first as a genius in mathematics, then as a genius in astrophysics. He did not *climb* the ladder of success—he ignored it altogether and *flew*. Higher and higher and higher he soared, 'til he was almost dizzy with triumph after triumph.

It was almost inevitable, he would muse later, that a storm would arrive to intercept his course. Only someone beyond mortality and the finite human mind could possibly enjoy perfect success.

The storm was harsh and unforgiving, and he was compelled to abandon his ambitions in the university. Instead, he was left to focus on his quieter but stronger accomplishments. He had risen from servant to king in a realm of shadows, and he concentrated upon expanding his kingdom. Conquest after conquest, he experienced nothing but victory on this plane of existence, for none could withstand—let alone contest—him.

He held his reign for many years, alone and unchallenged.

Then came a light that grew in radiance until it pierced his shadows, impeded his flight. Stronger and stronger the light grew, and became the first true threat he had ever faced. He attempted to extinguish the light—indeed, nearly quenched it—but it survived.

It survived, and he fell. He fell and attempted to pull the brilliant boy—for the light was a boy—with him.

He touched ground and stood against his foe, and they struggled on a great height. He attacked like a great bird of prey, swooping down upon the boy and tearing at him. His prey was weak, and he moved in for the kill...

Then he flailed at the edge, and the boy watched with something akin to vindication in his luminous eyes.

He fell.

He fell, and at last he realised that he had not flown in a very long time. He realised that he had always been falling, and now he would never fly again.

Quoth the detective, "Nevermore," his mind supplied ironically.

> *And the boy, never flitting, still is sitting, still is sitting*
> *On the cliff far above me;*

*And his eyes have all the seeming of an angel's that is
dreaming,*
*And the sunlight o'er him streaming throws his shadow
on the falls;*

*And my soul from out that shadow that lies floating on
the falls*
Shall be lifted—nevermore!

Day 19: A Father's Love

"I'll take that, Mrs. Hudson."

"Oh, bless you, Davy."

"Pardon me, gentlemen…"

"Careful now, Wig."

"'M all right!"

"This package is not labelled… Watson, you wrapped this?"

"Hmm? Oh, that is Colin's."

"Thank you."

Watson sighed and threw himself down on the settee while Holmes, Mrs. Hudson, and Davy Wiggins bustled around him. "This dinner grows larger and larger every year…"

"Because the Irregulars grow in number with each passing year," Holmes said easily, finishing off the label for Colin's gift and setting it with its fellows beneath the Christmas tree.

"At this rate, you shall have an organisation far exceeding what you or even Wiggins can handle," Watson warned, massaging his bad shoulder.

Wiggins had been passing the settee with the goose, but he halted and bent down. "Then we'll simply organise ourselves like the Yard," he said in a stage whisper. Watson laughed, saw the obligatory scowl Holmes gave, and laughed even harder.

"Mr. Holmes," Mrs. Hudson interjected, "how are we to fit *thirty-seven* boys in this room?"

"Obviously, we cannot," Holmes replied airily. "We shall fit them all between the sitting room and my bedroom; that will do."

"If you say so, sir." Mrs. Hudson looked somewhat less than convinced.

"I do," Holmes said firmly.

He was right. It ended up rather a tight fit, but they did manage.

Watson watched the boys eat and laugh, warm and able to fill their bellies for once. The Baker Street Irregulars were a diverse group in age, ethnicity, appearance, and personality. The Wiggins brothers were staunchly Anglo-Saxon, but Sean Youghal was purely Irish—and he was not the only Irish boy. Allen Rhys was one of the few Irregulars who were not street Arabs—more than that, he was actually the nephew of Lestrade's wife. Mrs. Lestrade's family was a rare blend of Welsh and Jewish. Jakez was Breton. Tommy was Italian. Nick was Russian.

Most of these boys were bound by poverty, and all by love. From the oldest to the youngest, they loved each other and they loved their father.

And their father loved them.

Watson saw it when he witnessed Holmes playing with the younger boys, boxing with the older ones, teaching them how to write, singing with the few songbirds of the group... He recalled the first time he'd seen Holmes embrace one of his Irregulars. Holmes was a man who cherished his privacy and his personal space, and Watson had expected his flat mate's back to stiffen when that limping little scarecrow had thrown his arms around the detective. To Watson's surprise, however, Holmes had returned the embrace fully.

Sherlock Holmes loved children, and they loved him. There was something timeless about his spirit, mature beyond his years and yet forever young, that endeared him to children, that allowed him to understand them, empathise with them. Watson had seen Holmes more at ease with children than with adults many times.

The gifts were practical, as they always were, but the boys were delighted. Watson laughed to see one of the recent recruits prance among his fellows, flinging his scarf this way and that. The doctor glanced up to see Holmes watching them all, his grey eyes soft and solemn. Wiggins rose from his position on the floor and stepped over one of the little ones to reach his mentor; he bent over and whispered something in Holmes's ear. Holmes quirked a little smile, shook his head, shrugged his shoulders. He navigated the moving sea of boys to reach his Stradivarius high on the bookcase, safe from grubby little hands.

The boys gamely tried to sing "Hark, the Herald Angels Sing," "Deck the Halls," "We Wish You a Merry Christmas," and "Silent Night." Wiggins did his utmost to conduct them all with his strong tenor, but to no avail. The result was an amusing ramble of different accents and pitches, but Holmes never faltered, leading them through song after song.

Watson caught Holmes's eye, and Holmes grinned. Watson smiled back at him.

The man who presented himself to the world as cold and unfeeling revealed himself to thirty-seven boys as a father who loved them deeply and thought the world of them. It was a legacy Watson knew would be remembered by the children of these children, and their children after them… And yet, Watson knew it was a legacy he could never publish.

Some things are too sacred to put into print.

Day 20: Sherlock's Twelve Days of Christmas

On the first day of Christmas,

My Boswell gave to me

A Norway spruce Christmas tree.

On the second day of Christmas,

My Boswell gave to me

Two small notebooks

And a Norway spruce Christmas tree.

On the third day of Christmas,

My Boswell gave to me

Three fountain pens,

Two small notebooks,

And a Norway spruce Christmas tree.

On the fourth day of Christmas,

My Boswell gave to me

Four commonplace books,

Three fountain pens,

Two small notebooks,

And a Norway spruce Christmas tree.

On the fifth day of Christmas,

My Boswell gave to me

Five gold tiepins,

Four commonplace books,

Three fountain pens,

Two small notebooks,

And a Norway spruce Christmas tree.

On the sixth day of Christmas,

My Boswell gave to me

Six silver cufflinks,

Five gold tiepins,

Four commonplace books,

Three fountain pens,

Two small notebooks,

And a Norway spruce Christmas tree.

On the seventh day of Christmas,

My Boswell gave to me

Seven revolver bullets,

Six silver cufflinks,

Five gold tiepins,

Four commonplace books,

Three fountain pens,

Two small notebooks,

And a Norway spruce Christmas tree.

On the eighth day of Christmas,

My Boswell gave to me

Eight sheets of foolscap,

Seven revolver bullets,

Six silver cufflinks,

Five gold tiepins,

Four commonplace books,

Three fountain pens,

Two small notebooks,

And a Norway spruce Christmas tree.

On the ninth day of Christmas,

My Boswell gave to me

Nine bottles of ink,

Eight sheets of foolscap,

Seven revolver bullets,

Six silver cufflinks,

Five gold tiepins,

Four commonplace books,

Three fountain pens,

Two small notebooks,

And a Norway spruce Christmas tree.

On the tenth day of Christmas,

My Boswell gave to me

Ten watercolours,

Nine bottles of ink,

Eight sheets of foolscap,

Seven revolver bullets,

Six silver cufflinks,

Five gold tiepins,

Four commonplace books,

Three fountain pens,

Two small notebooks,

And a Norway spruce Christmas tree.

On the eleventh day of Christmas,

My Boswell gave to me

Eleven cigarillos,

Ten watercolours,

Nine bottles of ink,

Eight sheets of foolscap,

Seven revolver bullets,

Six silver cufflinks,

Five gold tiepins,

Four commonplace books,

Three fountain pens,

Two small notebooks,

And a Norway spruce Christmas tree.

On the twelfth day of Christmas,

My Boswell gave to me

Twelve Irregulars drumming,

Eleven cigarillos,

Ten watercolours,

Nine bottles of ink,

Eight sheets of foolscap,

Seven revolver bullets,

Six silver cufflinks,

Five gold tiepins,

Four commonplace books,

Three fountain pens,

Two small notebooks,

And a Norway spruce Christmas tree.

XXX

"Confess now, Watson—Mycroft aided you."

"Well, perhaps a bit."

"I wonder what Lestrade would say if I committed fratricide?"

Day 21: The Toy

"Holmes?

"Holmes…

"Holmes!"

"Oh, confound it! *What*, Watson?"

"What on *earth* **is** that thing?"

"It is called a Celluloid Entertainment Console, Doctor. Mycroft says his department is testing them out as a method of building problem-solving skills."

"…I seeee… And you, ah, *need* aid in building problem-solving skills?"

"Don't be daft, man. It is a complex little machine with the most intriguing scenarios programmed into it."

"…*programmed.*"

"Yes."

"I see. It is… rather *loud.*"

"Ah, yes. Unfortunately, the inventors have yet to design volume control."

"…volume control."

"Quite so."

Ten minutes later...

"Holmes, I am trying to write—would you *please* stop playing with that thing?"

"*Celluloid Entertainment Console*, Watson. Oh, very well— I'll take it into my bedroom."

"Thanks awfully."

Twenty minutes...

"Half an hour. Half a bloody hour, and I am already being driven insane. This flat is not, as the Americans say, big enough for me and that cursed machine."

The next day...

"Watson, have you seen my Celluloid Entertainment Console?"

"Afraid I haven't, old man! Did you look downstairs?"

"No, but I shall do so now. I can't think where it might be..."

One minute later...

"...I'm sorry, Holmes, truly, but it was a matter of that toy or my sanity. I ask only that you not dispose of me as well once you realise what has happened."

Day 22: Far but Close

Dear Sherlock,

I dearly hope that my letter finds you and the Watsons well. Your brother has informed me that the good Doctor had departed with Kitchener's Army; I was surprised, but I should not have been. Dr. Watson has always been a soldier, first and foremost, has he not?

Young Godfrey wishes that he was a British citizen so that he might go to Europe. I thank God that he is not and that the U.S. of A. has had the sense to remain out of Europe's conflict, and yet I cannot help but feel that such a sentiment is terribly selfish of me. How dare I be relieved that my son cannot go to war when tens of thousands of mothers wish their sons had not? I fear, dear Sherlock. I fear for this, our children's, generation.

How fare the Watson children without their father? How fares Eileen? And, yes, Sherlock, how do *you* cope with the— pray God that it is temporary, only!—loss of your Boswell?

Will you still keep bees in Sussex, or is your return to London permanent? Mycroft would say only that you have done and are continuing to do services for king and country. I hope that you remain safe as you do so. The world has already been turned upside down enough; it need not lose one of the great heroes of Victoria's reign.

And speaking of heroes, I do believe that Cécile has developed an infatuation for you, thanks to Dr. Watson's stories. Never mind that you are old enough to be her father and might nearly have become such, given time—she is quite in love with gaslight, London Particulars, amateur detectives, and veteran doctors. The amateur detective holds her highest affection.

Forgive me for teasing you, dear, but it is true. I am not worried overmuch about it: because of her affection for you, she has developed certain high standards to expect in a suitor. In all likelihood, you are guarding her heart from falling for unworthy scoundrels, like the "King of Bohemia." May my little girl be wiser in her choices than her mother was.

Another thing I must thank you for, as if I did not already owe you enough. I know that you considered our debts balanced, but I do not. I needed stability in those few months as much as you did, perhaps more so. It is a grave thing for a mother to be alone in the world with her infant twins whilst abroad. For those happy few months, you did give my children something they needed desperately: a father's love. For that, you have my undying gratitude.

It is late now, so I shall close in a moment. I do not know when this letter shall reach you, so I shall wish you an early Merry Christmas. I hope it shall still be merry, this first Christmas of the War to End All Wars. (Do you truly believe that title? I cannot. It seems far too optimistic, perhaps even arrogant.)

May there still be joy in your home, and in the Watson's. And I remain

Yours most truly,

Irene Norton

XXX

"Uncle Sherlock, who is that letter from?"

"An old friend, Helen-girl. A dear old friend. You met her once, but you were too young to remember."

"Oh?"

"Do you remember your father's tale of The Woman? Well, I was reunited with her a few years later, on the Continent during those three years following Reichenbach..."

Day 23: A Friend in Need

"John, I need you more than your friend does. If this continues…"

"I understand, sir."

"Watson, I need you."

"Holmes, I cannot leave Henning in the lurch again. I shall certain lose my position, this time, and I am needed *here*. You saw for yourself the line of patients just beyond this door."

"But… Never mind. I shall… never mind. So sorry to have disturbed you, Watson."

"Holmes, you're hurt!"

"A trifle, really. Oh, Watson, come—I've had far worse than this."

"Considering that you were nearly killed by a bullet once, I cannot find that very comforting. Sit down."

"No! Watson, I cannot delay!"

"John?"

"Dr. Henning, sir."

"Is anything wrong?"

Watson. I need you.

I know.

"Sir, I must regretfully tender my resignation. My services are needed elsewhere."

Oh, Watson.

"John, really! Resignation and on such short notice!"

"My sincerest apologies for that, sir, but I truly am needed. Come, Holmes."

"But... John!"

XXX

"...Watson?"

"Yes, Holmes?"

"Do not think me blind to what this is costing you."

"Yes, well... You said you need me. You do not use that word often—I know that matters are important when you do."

"Well-reasoned, Watson."

"Besides..."

"Why are you smiling?"

"Oh, you idiot. You are my dearest, truest friend and the one man for whom I would drop everything to follow."

"…really?"

"Really, old fellow."

Christmas Eve: Together

The sound of voices in the sitting room, hushed but clarion to his sensitive ears, pulled him back to the land of the living.

Taking care to be quiet and, well, careful, Sherlock Holmes pushed himself up to a sitting position and slid out of bed. The floor was no less cold than when he had tried this earlier, but the sensation was not completely unwelcome. Still as unsteady as a newborn foal, he groped his way along the furniture until he'd reached the door. He heard the voices in the room beyond go silent as he turned the doorknob and pushed the door open.

He must have truly been a sight: still fairly mummified, half-dead beneath that, and standing on wobbling legs. But he was *standing*. He grinned tiredly at his astonished audience.

"Holmes!" Watson cried.

"Sherlock!" Mycroft and Mary exclaimed together. Sherlock was astonished to see his brother pale and considerably thinner than his wont, and he did not need his brain to be at full capability to know why. *Dear brother, I am so sorry.*

"What on *earth* are you doing out of bed?" Watson demanded, hazel eyes still wide with shock.

"Obviously, my insensitive brother wishes to give us a serious fright when he collapses from exhaustion," Mycroft said pointedly. Sherlock simply shook his head and did not protest when Mycroft assisted him towards his own armchair, into which he sank gratefully.

It was the first time in over a month that he had presided over his domicile from his throne. He felt nearly giddy with joy at being able to return to it.

"Thank you, brother mine," he murmured. He flashed the Watsons another grin, this one shorter-lived and even more tired than the first.

"Oh, Sherlock," Mary breathed. She rose uncertainly from the settee, then abandoned all hesitation and rushed forward to embrace him. "You are going to be all right—oh, thank God!"

"In time, at any rate," Sherlock agreed feelingly, wrapping his arms around her. He could not imagine how he must appear to her in his damaged state, but, apparently, she did not care. Mary was absolutely worthy to be the helpmeet of his dearest friend. "I have missed you, Mary," he whispered, returning her embrace with all the strength he could manage.

Mary pulled away and wiped at the tears falling from her large blue eyes. "I've missed *you*." She gave a self-conscious little laugh. "My apologies—I had not intended…"

"Shh." He put his finger on her lips. "It's all right."

She nodded and stood, backing away to let her husband step forward. "You left your bed just today?" said John.

Sherlock nodded, still amazed that he'd managed it.

Watson sighed and shook his head. "You are an idiot," he said flatly.

"I heartily concur, Doctor," Mycroft harrumphed.

Sherlock smiled slightly—*both* his brothers were visibly repressing smiles. He opened his mouth to retort, but he never had the chance to start. From his bedroom, he heard the sound of shattering glass and a *whoosh* that was all too familiar.

Adrenaline is a curious thing. Even when one is convalescing from a grave illness, adrenaline can grant the body enough strength to forget its exhaustion. Sherlock and Watson sprang from their chairs almost simultaneously, and, in his peripheral vision, Sherlock saw Mycroft taking Mary's hand and hurrying her to the door.

"Mycroft, get Mary and Mrs. Hudson out of the house!" Watson shouted.

"John!" Mary cried, right as Sherlock re-entered his bedroom. Flames licked at the rug, spread from a good old-fashioned torch.

"Good heavens," he heard Mycroft say.

"*Go,* Mycroft!" Sherlock shouted hoarsely. He raised his dressing gown to protect his nose and mouth as he grabbed the sheets off his bed. Watson was already beating at the fire with the blanket, and Sherlock joined him. It was a frantic rhythm— Sherlock would not allow his mind to calculate the consequences of a fire spreading throughout his rooms. It was unthinkable.

The room filled with smoke, and it was over nearly as quickly as it had begun.

His adrenaline expended, Sherlock collapsed against the bed, coughing uncontrollably. Watson lifted him up easily and bore him back out to the sitting room, laying him out on the settee. "Stay here," Watson said urgently, and then he was gone. Sherlock merely buried his face into one of the pillows, struggling to stop the coughs.

A minute later, Mycroft and Mary were back, with Mrs. Hudson in tow. "Oh, Mr. Holmes," his landlady half-sighed in that motherly tone she used so well.

"I'll fetch him some water," he heard Mary say.

Sherlock looked up to see Mycroft settle his depleted bulk into Sherlock's armchair. "Of all the ways to spend Christmas Eve…"

When Mary returned a moment later, her husband was with her. John leant over the back of the settee as Mary delivered a glass to the convalescent detective. "Thank you, dear," Sherlock said after gulping down the welcome water. "Well?" he added in an undertone to Watson.

"Wiggins is *not* going to be happy at a second assassin getting past his defences," Watson sighed. "I couldn't be certain, but I think I recognised the man as one of the lot that's tried to get into this house before. I only caught the back of him clearly as he fled."

Sherlock leant back and closed his eyes with a sigh. "Should have known—". He coughed. "Moriarty would have attempted arson as… as a way to finish me… if all else failed…"

"You've been scarcely lucid enough even to entertain such a notion," Watson said severely.

A wave of shame washed over the detective—he was coming to acknowledge that he had brought all this upon himself and had brought grief to the people around him. He draped his arm across his still-closed eyes, attempting to huddle down in the settee as if he could hide himself in disgrace from the world. "I know."

"Holmes." His Boswell's voice was gentle this time. "Moriarty won the first battle, not the war."

Mary's cry of delight brought their attentions back to the present. "Thank you so much, Mr. Holmes."

Sherlock opened his eyes and glanced from beneath his arm at his honorary sister, who was smiling down at a beautifully bound copy of *Idylls of the King* in her lap.

"Tennyson is much too flowery, Mycroft," Sherlock muttered.

Mary heard him, glanced up to meet John's eyes, and shook her head. "Never mind him, dear," Mrs. Hudson advised, smiling. "What is the book about?"

As Mary explained, Watson returned his attention to Sherlock and shook his head. "I don't think he shall try again tonight," the Doctor whispered. The others were busying themselves with the gifts beneath the tree, striving for a sense of normalcy. "For tonight, Holmes, let's enjoy this holiest of holidays."

Sherlock smirked wearily. "Poetic... as ever, Watson." The expression swiftly crumbled as a solemn sensation nagged at the back of his mind. "Do you know, I somehow feel as if... as if this is the last Christmas we shall enjoy together for... for quite a long time."

Even as the words came out of his mouth, he knew they were a mistake. Watson blanched. "Holmes, don't say that."

"My dear Watson, I am many things, but I am not prescient, despite what others may think. It is a... a vague intuition. Nothing more."

"I've always trusted your intuition."

Sherlock reached up and fondly patted Watson's hand. "Then trust this: no matter how far and how long we are separated, we shall always come back to each other. That is more than an intuition, my dear fellow—that is a promise."

They both remembered those words next Christmas, of course, when a decision made above a waterfall somewhere in Switzerland separated them. One wished desperately that a friend had not given his life for victory; the other wished that he had not walked away from his Boswell. Fires on the hearth reminded both of the flames that had attempted to ruin their last Christmas together.

Christmas Day: Family

John kept a tight hold on his two-year-old son and watched the womenfolk bustle about the Lestrades' kitchen and sitting room. The youngest Lestrade girl, Esther, was content to play dolls with Helen, despite the difference of four years in age. Lestrade and Wiggins were talking shop—in the months since Holmes's retirement, Davy Wiggins had become the new consultant of the older Yarders.

The Lestrade and Wiggins children were either playing or preparing the tables, which left John off to the side to avoid being bowled over. Little Sherlock Harold Watson was, for now, content to rest his head on his father's good shoulder and watch the goings-on.

Then John caught the sound of the front door opening, and a hearty *ho-ho-ho!* booming out. Sherlock shot up in John's arms, green eyes wide. "Fah-ther Cwiss-mass!" he cried, dropping out of his father's hold and darting away with the other young children. John chuckled and followed at a more sedate pace to find a rosy-cheeked, gift-laden Mycroft Holmes out in the hall, beset by a small army of children.

"You almost missed dinner, Mr. Claus," John called, grinning.

"*You* are as incorrigible as my brother," Mycroft retorted, trying to disentangle himself from the clutches of Sherlock Jr.

and little Ian Wiggins. He succeeded and waded through the children—all trying to get a look at the plethora of presents now littering the hall—to enfold John in a brotherly embrace. "Merry Christmas, John."

"Merry Christmas, Mycroft." John pulled away just enough to peer around the larger man's shoulder. "Do you know, I believe you outdid yourself this year?"

The elder Holmes shrugged expansively. "I have no immediate family to indulge aside from Sherlock, and the young fool certainly needs no indulgence from me." Seven years was apparently an eternity, and Mycroft would be calling his brother "young" when they were both in their dotage—if such a thing ever came to be. John had legitimate doubts. "And I do so enjoy the challenge of choosing gifts for everyone—quite a nice change from the stress of Whitehall."

John nodded his understanding, and then frowned as he noticed Helen standing on tiptoe to peer out the front window. She looked about as distressed as her four years would allow. "Helen, darling, what is the matter?"

She padded over to her father. "I thought *he* would come." She looked ready to cry.

Of course. John did not need to ask who *he* was. "Oh, sweetheart." He lifted her into his arms and held close. "Perhaps next Christmas."

Mycroft was watching them intently. "Helen," he said, gently, "would you like me to give you your gift now?"

Helen looked up and nodded wordlessly, brushing a tear away from her right cheek.

"Very well." Mycroft returned to the door, opened it, and whistled. A few moments later, the door swung open once more to reveal another tall figure, this one lean and black-clad with a grey scarf concealing much of his face.

The mirthful grey eyes, however, were unmistakeable.

Helen's eyes went round, and she leapt down to rush at the newcomer. "*Uncle Sherlock!*" She collided full-force with the thin legs, and the figure staggered backwards, laughing.

"Merry Christmas, Helen-girl!" he cried, pulling down his scarf and sweeping her up into his arms. Sherlock Holmes flung his free arm out in a theatrical wave and called, "Merry Christmas to all, and to all, a good day!"

Lestrade and Wiggins appeared around the corner, Wiggins hurrying forward to greet his former mentor. The Yarder merely leaned against the wall, folding his arms and casting a longsuffering look at John, who could only return a bewildered expression. Mycroft seemed to be quite satisfied.

The younger Holmes made his way through the gifts and children and now bore his namesake godson along with his goddaughter. He reached John and beamed. "Merry Christmas, Watson."

"Holmes," John murmured, studying his friend. The last time they'd seen each other had been in October—in Sussex, of course. When Holmes had left, he'd sworn… "You said you'd not come back."

The smile froze on the lean face. "Helen, Sherlock, dears, why don't you go help the other children deliver Uncle Mycroft's presents to the tree, hmm?" The pair murmured their assent and slid down, leaving two old friends facing each other. Mycroft had somehow slipped away without their notice, and Lestrade was occupied with the children.

"You came back."

"I did," Holmes said quietly. "And I did say that I would not come back."

"Then why did you?"

"Surely, my dear Watson, you must be familiar with my bad habit, after all these years."

"Which one?" Watson said drily.

Holmes gave him a look. "My bad habit of saying things which I regret later."

"Ah. *That* one."

"You are not making this easy."

"Have I any reason to do so?"

One dark eyebrow arched elegantly. "*Touché.*" Holmes shook his head. "My dear fellow, can you forgive me for that?"

Watson sighed. "*Why* did you come back?"

"Because the people whom I love are here."

John froze. It was most certainly not in Sherlock Holmes's nature to be so candid about his own emotions. "I beg your pardon?"

"The people whom. I love. Are here. Watson, do stop gaping as though you were a fish in a Billingsgate stall, there's a good fellow?"

John shook his head, freeing his mind to work again after the shock given it. "Holmes, I... I don't know what to say. Except that I am terribly glad you've come."

"I'm rather glad myself," Holmes ventured with a shy grin.

John chuckled and clapped him on the shoulder. "Come into the sitting room, old man. I think there are others who would like to wish you holiday greetings."

As they entered the sitting room arm in arm, they found Helen with her arms wrapped around Mycroft. "That was the bestest Christmas present *ever*, Uncle Mycroft," she said happily. "Thank you."

"Thank your present himself," Mycroft said, laughing. "Go on." He set the little girl down, who then came running back to the younger Holmes.

"Thank you, Uncle Sherlock!" she cried, wrapping her arms around his legs.

Sherlock Holmes smiled down at her. "You're welcome, Helen-girl. Merry Christmas."

"Merry Christmas!"

Watson squeezed Holmes's shoulder and repeated, "Merry Christmas."

Day 26: Helpmeet

"Good heavens!"

"Mary, you…"

"Yes."

"He's…"

"Alive."

"Oh. Good."

From her sitting position on… well, on a prone criminal, Mary Watson blinked innocently up at her husband and her honorary brother (in-law). She folded her hands demurely in her lap and raised an inviting eyebrow. John lowered himself to the floor—mindful of his bad leg—to check Gates as best he could with his wife perched on the prisoner's back.

"He is handcuffed," Holmes felt the need to point out.

"Yes, he is."

"With my handcuffs."

"Yes."

Holmes resisted the urge to knead his forehead. "How did you get them?"

"I lifted them off of you," she said easily. "Davy taught me."

John's jaw hit his collar.

Holmes continued to resist the urge to knead his forehead, despite the vicious headache forming there. When he'd dropped in on the Watsons' Christmas dinner with a plea for Watson's help, he had not counted on getting Mary in the bargain. But even he had to succumb to a five-foot-three powerhouse with a stern governess's gaze and a voice to match.

Somehow, in the warehouse they'd been searching, she'd slipped off without either man noticing. Holmes found that fact alone to be profoundly embarrassing, and to compound his embarrassment… One minute, they were looking for Gates; the next minute, a commotion broke out in the building, followed by a tremendous crash. Finally realising that Mary was gone, they'd run toward the source of the noise, only to find Mrs. Watson sitting placidly on a handcuffed criminal with a bleeding skull.

Those clandestine martial arts lessons had obviously paid off.

John cleared his throat. "Well."

"Well?"

John flashed his friend an awkward grin. "You did say 'most useful' and 'decided genius.'"

Holmes had the grace to blush.

Mary glanced between them questioningly. "I beg your pardon?"

"Never mind," the men chimed together.

"Not worth repeating," Holmes added. Not at all worth repeating a conversation that had very nearly driven a wedge between himself and his Boswell, thank you very much.

"Well," John said again.

"Well?"

"Shouldn't we hail the nearest constable?"

"Go ahead, dear," Mary told him, settling more comfortably in her makeshift cushion.

John weighed for a moment the ramifications of bringing a PC to this little tableau, with his own wife having taken down the criminal, and sighed. Convention be hanged, in this instance. Mary had done a good day's work.

He looked up at Holmes and bit down a laugh at the detective's bewildered expression. The best of women are not to be trusted, indeed!

He waited until he was out of earshot before he laughed heartily at their ludicrous situation. What a Christmas!

Day 27: One of Those Days

Geoffrey Michael Lestrade started his day with the discovery that Jones was down with influenza. What was cause for the other inspectors' sympathy was cause for Lestrade's frustration, for he found himself inundated with Jones's caseload. Gregson drawled some remark about "nobody but the best" getting the largest caseload, his tone arrogant and condescending but his posture radiating relief.

Of course, the Chief Inspector's "favourite son" doesn't have to worry about being flooded with work, Lestrade thought darkly as he stomped into his office.

Bradstreet, bless the big oaf, offered to take some of the load off Lestrade's shoulders. What he ended up doing was knocking over a stack of cases-to-be-filed-away. It was the sort of stack that fell under the much-too-high-to-be-safe category, and Lestrade had long been meaning to take care of it. He'd simply not had the time for the past several weeks, so the stack had grown to a precarious height on the desk.

Roger had apologised profusely and attempted to help Lestrade pick them back up... then Police Sergeant Manning had darted into the office to inform Lestrade that his boys had made an arrest but lost the criminal. The criminal in question was one Isa Vance, whom Lestrade had been working to apprehend for the past two weeks for a jewel theft. Constable Parsons was now being treated by Dr. Watson for a concussion.

All this before nine o'clock.

Lestrade was nearly ready to give *himself* a concussion to escape it all.

But policemen have their responsibilities, and they stick to them. That had been Lestrade's mantra for two decades, and, by George, he wasn't abandoning it now.

Still, he was sorely tempted when he received a telegram from Mr. Know-It-All Sherlock Bloody Holmes, who required search and arrest warrants. Lestrade couldn't even *consider* refusing—he owed Holmes too many cases to turn down a request for a favour. Ha. Less a request and more calling him on a debt. Several, if one was to get purely technical. *Fool amateur detectives and their two-edged largess.*

"I'm certain he needs them, sir," Hopkins offered tentatively. "He..."

The boy would've been better off keeping his mouth shut, for Lestrade shot him a glare that could have flayed a man alive. The senior detective then promptly sent Hopkins *(crying to his hero)* to Baker Street with said warrants.

PC Harry Murcher attempted to help Lestrade with his impromptu snowfall, but the big man ended up making the mess worse. (As Lestrade knew he would, but Murcher had been one of his mates when *Lestrade* was patrolling his own beat years ago. Who was he to refuse such an old friend?)

Davy Wiggins, of all people, dropped by after his English lessons with Lestrade's wife, Annie, to inform him that his eldest boy Jeremy was coming down with a cold. Wiggins insisted on paying for the cough syrup himself, and Lestrade found it difficult to argue with a pair of bright blue eyes that reminded him uncomfortably of a certain pair of bright grey ones...

To top it all off, Lestrade was called in for a meeting with *Mycroft* "British Government" Holmes. (Not that he would ever say it or even knew it for an indisputable fact, but—contrary to the younger Holmes's opinions—he was neither blind nor stupid.) Mycroft ended the meeting by apologising for pulling Lestrade away from his duties on such a bad day—certainly, no Holmesian genius need apply: the inspector knew he looked as harried and world-weary as he felt. Whitehall's Mr. Holmes then suggested that Lestrade get Baker Street's Mr. Holmes to help him out; Lestrade thanked him for the suggestion and left.

As if he would ask Sherlock Holmes for yet *another* favour when he was already up to his ears in debt! That wasn't even counting the fact that Annie's tuition fees for Wiggins's lessons were coming straight out of the madman's pocketbook!

At the end of the day, Hopkins, Holmes, Watson, and—did wonders never cease—Isa Vance showed up at the Yard. Vance was promptly escorted to a cell, Hopkins slunk off to avoid his superior, and Holmes assured Lestrade once again that his name need not be mentioned in conjunction with the case. The amateur strode off in high spirits, leaving his personal physician standing beside his erstwhile personal caretaker.

"As if I can actually lie that blatantly in the report," Lestrade muttered sourly.

Watson patted his shoulder more out of *empathy* than *sympathy*. "Lestrade."

"Yes, Doctor?"

"There comes a time in a man's life when, at the end of the day, he has to seek solace in a public establishment by liquid means."

The young veteran sounded as if he was at that point in time, himself. Lestrade cocked an eyebrow. "One of *those* days, eh?"

"The same for you, yes?"

"However did you deduce that?"

The two men shared a long look. "I hear The Crooked Arrow carries an excellent black cider," Watson suggested.

Lestrade felt a grin creep up on him and grab hold. "Actually, John, I was thinking of something a bit stronger…"

Day 28: A Changing Age

Sherlock Holmes, a gentleman born and bred, smoked neither pipe nor cigarette in the presence of a lady. But when, in 1902, John Watson brought his two-year-old daughter to 221B to visit her godfather after that sordid business with Baron Gruner, father and daughter found the sitting room engulfed in a haze of smoke. Helen hardly had time to cough before Watson slammed the door shut again, eliciting a cry from inside.

They were accosted on the kerb by a still very convalescent detective, who apologised profusely.

From that day on, Holmes confined three-pipe problems and all such smoking to his bedroom. His Boswell and his Boswell's family were worth it.

XXX

It was a handy practise. When the Watsons visited him in Sussex or when he began to visit *them* in London, he confined his smokes to the bedroom and the outdoors. It was not at all easy. He found his fingers twitching for a pipe or a cigarette, and he could not sate his craving unless he retreated.

XXX

After several years of training himself to go without at intervals, he found himself put to the test.

In America.

Altamont was a cocksure, slightly batty fellow who smoked only the finest cigarettes and shunned pipes altogether. Holmes himself was surprised to find that trait in his role, but he endured it as best he could. He scarcely ever dared to smoke his beloved clay pipe unless he was absolutely certain he would not be disturbed.

XXX

Holmes's undercover work at last came to a close, and it was with great relief that he shared a quiet pipe with Watson now and then at the start of that horrible August. When Watson left with the first wave of Kitchener's Army, Holmes could not bring himself even to *look* at his pipe, for it reminded him of his absent friend.

XXX

He spent very little time in 221B. Room 40 claimed most of his daytime hours, and, when he wasn't in Whitehall, he was either at the Diogenes Club, Mycroft's flat, the Watsons' house, or the Lestrades' house. Only in that last location was he allowed to smoke, and it was always a vast relief to do so.

Either Lestrade had gone soft or Holmes had, because they found they got on with each other quite well these days.

XXX

Then came the nerve-wracking year of 1918 and, with it, the news that Lieutenant-Colonel John H. Watson of the RAMC was missing. Sherlock Holmes and a now eighteen-year-old Helen Watson set off to scour the Continent. Holmes would have much preferred that she stay behind, but he could not triumph over Watsonian stubbornness in Helen any more than he could with John.

Heedless of the presence of a young lady, Holmes would puff enough smoke to rival a Victorian factory. That is, he did so until Helen put her foot down and forbade her godfather from using his pipe. Holmes complied, knowing that he had indeed gone soft and thinking of how much she favoured her father. He could very easily imagine Helen delivering a lecture on cocaine with every bit as much passion as John had.

It was just as well. In the trenches, smoking could be a liability.

XXX

The years following the war were difficult for everyone. Sherlock Holmes had his own personal issues—in the mid-'20s, he discovered that he was developing lung cancer. John and Helen were adamant that he quit smoking; John was quitting, himself.

It was torturous—in some ways, worse than cocaine withdrawal had ever been. Holmes even found himself subjected to some of the same symptoms. The worst of it was when his fingers would stray to his pocket or to the mantel in search of tobacco that was not there. The Persian slipper remained, but it was empty. The pipe rack had disappeared, courtesy of Helen.

The Watsons tried to fill the void left in their menfolk's lives with more time spent together as a family. Silent movies, parks, games... anything to keep John's and Sherlock's minds off of what they were giving up.

Helen helped tremendously. Married for several years now to Lestrade's youngest son, she had two children and one on the way. She regarded her children as having *three* grandfathers: John Watson, Geoffrey Lestrade, and Sherlock Holmes. Not a week passed that Holmes did not visit his goddaughter and her family, and he was ever grateful for Helen's love and encouragement.

XXX

When Sherlock Holmes died, neither waterfall nor vengeful criminal was involved. He died in his Helen's arms at the age of seventy-nine, his heart simply giving out. One doctor attributed it to long-term smoking finally catching up with him, but Helen knew the truth.

Sherlock Holmes had lived the last few months of his life with a heart broken by his dearest friend's death. He was ready to go—he had told Helen as much. And she knew that her father had received into his arms the best and wisest man he'd ever known.

Day 29: The Warrior a Child

She saw him that night, as she had seen him so many nights before.

He flashed her his famous not-quite-grin and tipped his cloth cap even as she called out his name. His once-boyish face was now grey and drawn and aged beyond his years—his grey eyes were bright but haunted with memories of great pain. Then he turned, as he always did, and strode away slowly, as if his back were bent by a burden almost greater than he could bear.

She watched as he climbed grassy hills and rocky heights, his invisible burden seeming to grow weightier with each step. Before long, he was nearly crawling rather than climbing, his hands and legs slipping far too often and collapsing him to the ground. He was torn, battered, bloodied, but still he pressed on.

He pressed on 'til he reached a vast waterfall. There, it was as if his burden rolled away, and he stood tall and unbowed, an erect silhouette against the rushing water like a monument of some great king. Eyes closed, he threw his head back and raised his hands to the sky as if returning to life and glorying in it.

Then came the dark figure. She could not make out its face—darkness seemed to go before it and surround it, a chill presence commanding fear.

The dark figure sprang at him, and he struggled in its hold. He had yet to regain his strength, had yet to recover, and so he was slower and weaker than his wont. A desperate anger burned in his eyes, and she saw his determination to see justice done, no matter the cost.

The dark figure lost its footing on the edge of the cliff, and it pulled him off with it. She saw the beloved grey eyes widen, saw the lips part to form a wordless cry. She saw them fall together, enemies in life, partners in death, limbs flailing as they fell with impossible slowness. Then they disappeared, together, into the mist rising from the lake at the bottom of the falls.

His cry rang in her ears as she jerked to wakefulness. She buried her face in her hands and sobbed. How long would she be tormented by these nightmares of her boy dying? She hadn't even seen him before he left for the Continent again; she'd never had the chance to say goodbye.

At least Dr. Watson had been with him up to the last few hours!

As Rose Hudson scrubbed her face clean of tears, she cast her mind back to the early days. Sherlock Holmes had indeed been the worst lodger in London, and Dr. Watson had been the darling of the pair. But, much as she adored the dear doctor, it was the younger, more difficult of her lodgers that had stolen her heart.

Denied the ability to bear children and deprived of her husband, her longing for motherhood had been fulfilled, in part, by a strange man-child with large, bright eyes. She had seen past the dazzling intellect, the kinglike authority, the childish callousness … she'd looked past it all and seen a soul starved for affection, not unlike a lost little boy.

So she'd given him all the affection she could.

Oh, there'd been times—many times—that she could cheerfully have walloped him in the broomstick, but nothing he could have done would ever have made her stop loving him. Under the doctor's open friendship and her more subtle affection, the young detective's spirit slowly but surely blossomed. She'd watched his relationship with Mary Watson change from one of near-resentment to open, brotherly regard. In the past two years, he had grown into a man of whom she could be truly proud, a man who used both his head and his heart.

In many ways, he was the son that she could never have.

And, oh, how terribly she missed her boy.

Day 30: Through the Fire

I never knew my father. My mother was an actress, and theatre was all I knew, growing up. I styled my mum's hair, applied her stage makeup, helped her with her costumes. She, in return, showered me with affection.

I loved Mum, but… with all the fire in my soul, I wished I could have had the chance to love my father, as well.

XXX

I loved to learn. I taught myself more by reading books than any of my tutors ever did, my eager young mind absorbing all that I read. Chemistry held my fancy for a while, and Mum had to forbid me from "experimenting" with the makeup. But what truly captured my imagination was the Italian Renaissance, the romance of the period, the gorgeous art of imaginative souls.

Female artists were a rare breed, but I was determined to make my way into the art world somehow.

XXX

I was sixteen when I found work at an art studio. One of the artists had gushed over me, decreeing me to be a perfect model. I was proud to bring home my own wages, though I longed to sketch and paint as the men did.

But female artists were a rare breed.

XXX

Eventually, I gave up the studio. Being surrounded by the tools of the trade and unable to do so much as *touch* them tortured me. I had a voice flexible enough to pitch both soprano and contralto, and I decided to use it.

It was during my successful tenure as a singer that I met him.

XXX

He was much older than I, but ever so charming and gentlemanly. No man had ever treated me as a lady before, and this man did. I was soon visiting his home… and his bedchambers.

I would later curse the day we first set eyes upon each other.

XXX

I fled the beautiful house, weeping bitter, angry tears but taking care that the saltwater did not run down to touch my marred skin. I was disfigured now, still fair of face and form but bearing a large swath of acid-eaten skin. I knew I would lose my job, and I had no notion of where to go next.

I vowed then that my once-loved baron would pay.

XXX

This man was different. He was a gentleman and he acted it, but he was different all the same. I couldn't quite put my finger on it. Of course I'd heard of him—who hadn't? I'd spent my girlhood with *The Strand*. But where the doctor's hazel eyes held curiosity, *his* large grey eyes held compassion. Somehow, he knew; given his reputation, I supposed I shouldn't be surprised.

I still wanted revenge, but… after beholding those keen grey eyes, my heart wanted something more.

XXX

The deed was done. I'd flung the acid at my former lover, revenging myself and ensuring that the world would at last see this man for the monster he was. But before I fled, my green eyes met a pair of tired grey ones.

Those eyes bore understanding and utterly no condemnation. I fled.

XXX

Hyde's Park, 1915

I closed my eyes and inhaled my first true breath of spring. Winter had been long and hard, and it seemed that all of Europe must have been longing for the warmth of spring. After several terrible months of war with no end in sight, the world needed some cheer, fleeting though it might be.

My eyes flew open as a small body hurled into my legs, collapsing me to the grass. "Sorry, ma'am!" a small voice piped. I looked up to see a contrite little girl with hair nearly as red as my own.

"Maureen, do watch where you're running!" a boy's voice chided. The owner ran up into view, and I could have sworn that he looked familiar.

"There now, no harm done," I smiled, pushing myself back onto my feet. "But be more careful next time, love," I added to the little girl.

My own daughter, Laura, came running up. "Mum, are you all right?"

I laughed. "I'm fine, dear. Laura, meet my little attacker, Maureen." Maureen looked as though she were only a year or two younger than eight-year-old Laura.

The two were soon chatting, and Maureen's brother watching with a resigned air. "Surely you don't come here alone," I said aside to him.

"Oh, no. Our uncle is here with us—somewhere." The boy grinned. "Well, I say 'uncle,' but he's really our godfather."

I smiled again. "Do you know, I would say you remind me of someone, but I can't say who it might be?"

The boy's grin grew wider, his cheeks dimpling and his hazel eyes sparkling. "People do say that about me," he confided conspiratorially. Despite my confusion, I had to laugh—he was a little charmer and no mistake.

"Hamish, Maureen?"

I froze. I knew that voice, though it had been thirteen years since last I heard it.

Throwing me another mirthful glance, the boy lifted his head and called, "Over here, Uncle!"

A tall figure came into sight from around a high cluster of blossoming bushes. "Ah!" He lifted his walking stick in salute as he strode our way.

I could not believe my eyes. Sherlock Holmes.

Maureen and Laura paid him no heed, but Hamish's eyes darted back and forth impishly between me and the Great Detective. Of course. No wonder the boy looked familiar; he was the son of Dr. John Watson.

"Good morning, Mr. Holmes," I breathed, having regained enough composure to manage speech.

"Miss W—I suppose I must not say that," he corrected himself, glancing significantly at my wedding band. His grey eyes were surprised but pleased. "Congratulations."

"Thank you." I managed a smile next, and nodded at Laura. "My daughter, Laura."

He glanced at Laura and Maureen, still talking, and shrugged. "She appears to be engage at the moment." His expression was quite impassive, but those grey eyes danced— then grew solemn as he turned to face me fully. "Life seems to have treated you well," he said quietly.

I realised that Hamish had slipped off without my noticing, and nodded at the observation. "I found me a good man," I murmured. "Laura came along a year later, and…" I heaved a sigh, feeling a small, familiar ache in my chest. "He left with Kitchener's Army."

His expression grew pensive. "As did the good Doctor."

"I'm sorry." The words themselves were empty, but he understood.

He seemed to pull his mind away from the Western Front long enough to manage a small smile. "Even so, I am glad that you found happiness… Kitty."

New Year's Eve: Tradition

"Sherlock?"

"Yes, Mary?"

In lieu of a reply, Mary held up a sprig of...

"Mistletoe." Sherlock Holmes raised an eyebrow, instantly on his guard. "Mary, Christmas was a week ago."

"Yes, and it was rather an unforgettable one," Mary said drily. Sherlock had the grace to blush. "But this is not for Christmas," she continued. "Don't you know that it is tradition for mistletoe to be used between friends on New Year's Eve?"

The other eyebrow joined the first. "No, I did not." Perhaps he should consider storing holiday customs in his brain attic, after all, if Mary was to insist upon following them...

"Well..."

"Well?"

Mary was giving him her very best "exasperated teacher" expression. She lifted the mistletoe above her head and cleared her throat. Oh, was she really going to insist upon... She gave him a hopeful look. Yes, she was.

Five-foot-three with enormous blue eyes. Watson truly had not stood a chance.

"Very well," Holmes sighed, striding forward and placing a chaste kiss upon Mary's lips.

"…Holmes? Mary?"

At the sound of his friend's voice, Holmes shot straight up and whirled about to face the man. "Watson!"

The doctor looked perplexed. "What on earth were you two doing?"

Holmes belatedly realised that Mary had slipped away. "Your lovely wife had talked me into fulfilling a New Year's tradition," he explained, making a mental note to pay Mary back later for abandoning him to her husband. Nothing serious, of course—only mildly annoying.

Watson's perplexed expression grew—what on earth was the matter? "With… mistletoe?"

An uncomfortable feeling formed in Holmes's stomach. "Yes."

The hazel eyes widened, and Watson assumed that deadpan expression that Holmes knew from long experience meant his friend was struggling not to laugh. That uncomfortable feeling expanded exponentially. "Holmes. Mistletoe has absolutely nothing to do with celebrating the New Year—it is a tradition for Christmastime only."

Holmes felt his mouth slacken even as his cheeks burned. Watson lost control completely and staggered backwards, making undignified sounds somewhere between laughter and *giggles*.

She'd tricked him. Mary Watson had *tricked* Sherlock Holmes.

Watson continued to spasm with hilarity. "I suppose you shall have to say now that you've been bested by three men and *two* women!" he managed to gasp out.

Holmes responded in the only manner he could—by lobbing a pillow at his insufferable friend's face. Watson ducked and fell onto his settee, still caught in that obnoxious mixture of laughter and giggles. Holmes growled. "Watson! Pull yourself together, man!"

Watson merely clutched at his sides and started to choke on his mirth. Served him right.

Well, Holmes was not going to stand for this. No, sir—he was not to be bested by a five-foot-three former governess. It was time that Mary Watson discovered to what lengths Sherlock Holmes could take a prank. He withdrew his black clay pipe from his pocket, filled it with tobacco, and lit it. This was a matter worthy of his oldest and trustiest pipe.

And, with any luck, it would be fun.

Finis

Also from MX Publishing

A young girl's snowman has gone missing. Where can it have gone? There is only one man who can help. Sherlock Holmes, the most famous detective in the world.

Sherlock Holmes and The Missing Snowman brings together one of the UK's leading children's illustrators, Rikey Austin (creator of Alice's Bear Shop) and David Ruffle, author of several bestselling Sherlock Holmes thrillers, novellas and compilations. Rikey and David are both from the idyllic seaside town of Lyme Regis, a setting which has inspired this delightful children's book.

www.mxpublishing.com

Also from MX Publishing

Winners of the 2011 Howlett Literary Award (Sherlock Holmes book of the year) for '**The Norwood Author**'

From one of the world's largest Sherlock Holmes publishers dozens of new novels from the top Holmes authors around the world.

www.mxpublishing.com

Including our bestselling short story collections

'Lost Stories of Sherlock Holmes' and 'The Outstanding Mysteries of Sherlock Holmes'.

New in 2012 [Novels unless stated]:
Sherlock Holmes and the Plague of Dracula
Sherlock Holmes and The Adventure of The Jacobite Rose [Play]
Sherlock Holmes and The Whitechapel Vampire
Holmes Sweet Holmes
The Detective and The Woman: A Novel of Sherlock Holmes
Sherlock Holmes Tales From The Stranger's Room
The Sherlock Holmes Who's Who
Sherlock Holmes and The Dead Boer at Scotney Castle
A Professor Reflects on Sherlock Holmes [Essay Collection]
Sherlock Holmes of The Lyme Regis Legacy
Sherlock Holmes and The Discarded Cigarette [Short Novel]
Sherlock Holmes On The Air [Radio Plays]
Sherlock Holmes and The Murder at Lodore Falls

Also from MX Publishing

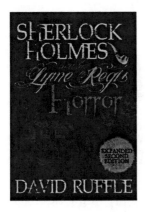 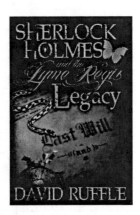

Sherlock Holmes and The Lyme Regis Horror and the sequel
Sherlock Holmes and The Lyme Regis Legacy

Sherlock Holmes – Tales from the Stranger's Room

An eclectic collection of writings from twenty Holmes writers.

www.mxpublishing.com

Also from MX Publishing

Sherlock Holmes Travel Guides

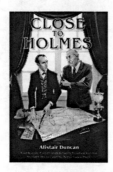 

And in ebook (stunning on the iPad) an interactive guide

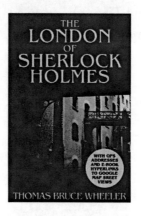

400 locations linked to Google Street View.

www.mxpublishing.com

Also from MX Publishing

Cross over fiction featuring great villans from history

and military history Holmes thrillers

 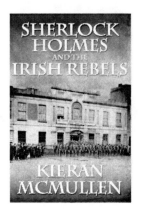